Praise from Readers of *Small Lies*:

This beautifully written collection of short stories profoundly touches on many aspects of the human experience. The characters are so well described that they jump off the pages and make you feel and identify with their growth, struggles, joys, prejudices, and triumphs. Catherine Gentile's story telling ability is seamlessly coupled with the exploration of the essence of the characters. The timeless nature of the issues, emotions, and relationships are penned in a thoughtful, sensitive, poignant and sometimes raw manner that grab your attention and won't let go long after the end of the story. I thoroughly enjoyed and highly recommend this collection.

—Richard Rudnansky, USA

Small Lies is a collection of short stories whose imagery and imagination surround you with hope as the characters master the challenges they face. Their stories will captivate you, will have you thinking about their courage and determination for days, and provide the reader a way to tap into their own resiliency. Catherine Gentile is a compassionate and articulate writer whose style draws you in and keeps your attention throughout.

—Sarah and Harvey Berman,USA

Catherine Gentile has given us carefully developed characters who launch themselves within situations that span a heart-capturing range of themes and settings. Her thought-provoking collection of short stories is a joy to read and think about.

—Joan Erickson, USA

Small Lies is the most tender and beautifully written short story collection that I have ever read. Catherine Gentile puts her heart and soul into conveying her characters' innermost feelings, their weaknesses, their strengths, and their secrets. In each and every story, you discover subtle meanings and words of wisdom that make each of them complete and fulfilling. Do yourself a favour—read it!

—Ida Egede Winther, Denmark

Do you remember a single defining moment that changed the course of your life? It was a moment you built upon years of existence. It was the moment you decided to be your true self. In *Small Lies*, Catherine Gentile has given us stories of these moments, very much like a butterfly escaping its cocoon. Her writing is descriptive; it sweeps the reader along as if riding a tide. These tales evoke many emotions, among them admiration, anger, love, and also astonishment at the failings of some people. Catherine has a command of words that is at times lyrical and poetic. Her grasp of different cultures, times and places is impressive to say the least! Savor these glimpses of humanity. You will not regret it!

—Judith Matthew,USA

Small Lies is a collection of short stories, beautifully written by Catherine Gentile. It gives us a mature and realistic account of human relationships within the social hardships and sometimes intolerance. Each story is different, thought provoking, and reflects her sensibility and perceptiveness. The book is a fascinating and intellectual read, which results in understanding many attitudes.

—Pamela Milne, Portugal

Deception is a shroud used to hide from painful truths. Catherine Gentile's use of engaging and believable characters and cultures in *Small Lies*, carries the reader on a journey of exploration in how such deception complicates and enslaves rather than provide protection from discomfort.

—Marcia Dedekian, USA

SMALL LIES

A Collection of Short Stories

Catherine Gentile

BookLocker
Saint Petersburg, Florida

PRINT ISBN: 978-1-64718-576-3
EPUB ISBN: 978-1-64718-577-0
MOBI ISBN: 978-1-64718-578-7

Published by BookLocker.com, Inc., St. Petersburg, Florida.

Printed on acid-free paper.

The characters and events in this book are fictitious. Any similarity to real persons, living or dead, is coincidental and not intended by the author.

BookLocker.com, Inc.
2020

First Edition

"Thomas's Bench" was originally published in *The Ledge*; "Buonma Song Youg O'Reilly" in *The Chaffin Journal*; "A Teaspoon of Perfection" in the anthology, *Hello, Goodbye*; "Whisper Notes" in *Kaleidoscope*; "Woven Butterflies" in *The Briar Cliff Review*; "Moon Tide Prayer" in *American Fiction, Volume 11: The Best Previously Unpublished Short Stories*.

Library of Congress Cataloging in Publication Data
Gentile, Catherine
Small Lies by Catherine Gentile
Library of Congress Control Number: 2020908721

In memory of Dad,
who told me my first stories

Also by Catherine Gentile:

The Quiet Roar of a Hummingbird

The Caregiver's Journey: Tools, Tips, Provisions:
An Ebook

Sunday's Orphan, available fall, 2021

SMALL LIES

CONTENTS

THOMAS'S BENCH

Thomas stands at the edge of his wife's Zen garden surveying the damage. A downed birch has gouged the earth, spilling leaves, flattening newly planted rhododendrons, creating chaos. Garden mold, once secured beneath a carpet of landscaping paper and pebbles, breezes upward, curls his broad nostrils into a sneeze. Thomas turns toward the window to see if Millie's watching, then lifts the hem of his T-shirt, wipes his nose, wishes he didn't have allergies and asthma. Between the two, he sniffles constantly. This annoys Millie; it always has. She likes her people well-mannered and things tidy, in order, like the flow of grainy lines she keeps so carefully raked. Not like this mess.

But the randomness of the granite nuggets appeals to Thomas, delights him even, although he isn't about to let on to Millie. With the guys in his support group maybe, the one he has yet to tell her about. Unemployed Executives, or RPM, as the guys dubbed it. Recovering Power Men. My reality, he thinks, running his fingers along a branch that's jammed into the fieldstone wall, is more like this than Millie suspects.

Sweat glistens on his round face, glasses glide toward the bulb of his nose, his wide biceps contract. He begins the work of disconnecting the branch from its trunk, knows the only merciful thing to do is to cut the once-lofty birch into pieces. If it sits on the damp ground, the stringy yellow interior will gorge itself with moisture, then rot. He saws, exploding the first burst of tension and positions himself to jump out of the way before he severs the branch. Otherwise, it'll spring back and slap him hard.

"My beautiful garden," Millie says, from the other side of the patio doors. The sun has yet to filter through the sagging spruce boughs, and the morning light shadows her honey-colored skin. "All that work—I hate starting over."

Thomas lifts his wire-rimmed frames, wipes his face with his handkerchief, while moisture from his thick chest wicks into twin stains on his shirt and his damp belly presses against his belt. "I've called McEnnary's Nursery. They'll cut the trunk and haul it away. But don't let them touch these." He points to the branches he's stacked by the wall. "I want them for a project," he says, with an easy confidence he hasn't heard since he was a boy, long before Grandma Betsy insisted he lose his black Southern drawl. "You can't talk that way if you're going to fit in," she said, dabbing at his soft, round sounds, soaking them up and away.

What would his exacting grandmother say if she were alive today? Determined to prove himself an exceptional first black CFO, he screwed up big time, let the expansion he directed outpace cash flow. Almost blotted Winston-Harding Financial Services of New England out of existence. Fortunately for the company, an underling, jealous of Thomas's success, reviewed his accounting practices with the CEO. Shortly after, she reassigned Thomas to the satellite office on the other side of town. Corporate gulag. From there, he read her smoke signals: Temporary lapse in hiring judgment...Recovered senses, maneuvering for same to happen with losses...Highly delicate, must not, repeat, not cause alarm with investors or within black community. Within two weeks, he shoved his severance package, along with his belongings, into his trunk. That was exactly one year ago today. From then on, he had filled his days with new activities. And never told Millie.

"You're going to be late for work," Millie says, her small head bowing to meet her coffee cup. "I've got a busy day, too."

Their large house had that empty quiet the kids leave behind after they've packed and gone to camp. There'd been a time, not long ago, when Millie and Thomas would have come into the kitchen to make coffee only to chase each other giggling up the stairs, hop on their four-poster bed, ride it 'til it creaked. Until they produced the same brazen sounds that had drifted from the whorehouses behind Melton Street where Thomas had lived with his grandmother in Atlanta.

"Feel good to work outside?" Millie asks, pouring him coffee.

He holds up the blister on his right hand and nods. "I have one of these to prove it." His voice has a fullness to it, so different from the hollow CFO noises he's made these last five years. He closes his eyes and slurps his coffee, feels her studying him.

"What are you going to do with those branches?" she asks, her words coming out fast, jockeyed perhaps, by her next thought.

"Build a bench for your garden." He watches Millie grimace as if he'd fed her an aspirin.

"A homemade bench in a formal garden. You think that'll work?"

"Does it have to?" The more he thinks about it, the more he likes the idea of testing his concentration, craftsmanship and honesty. In two of the three, he scores off the charts; about honesty—he isn't willing to say just yet.

"McEnnary's Nursery sells benches. Why don't we buy one?"

"I said I want to make it." He quickly adds, "I haven't done any woodworking in a while. It'll be relaxing." He watches her eyes for a flicker, one that recognizes his apology, doesn't take offense. He isn't disappointed.

"I have a design in mind, like the benches my grandmother and I used to sell to our neighbors." He pauses for a moment. "Remember when we were that poor?" Thomas's voice fades; he wheezes, pulls out his inhaler and squirts it in his mouth.

"I'd rather not." Millie rolls up the sleeves on the white silk robe he'd bought two years ago when he was in Tokyo on business. As soon as he landed a salaried position, Thomas started buying her presents. Little things at first: flowered notepaper, a box of licorice, a silver necklace with a butterfly. Later, as his degree from Wharton began paying off, a trip to the Swiss Alps, a BMW, their twelve-room home in the Berkshires. Each an antidote to the memory of Grandma Betsy handing him his first pair of new leather shoes the morning he left for college.

"I can't believe you're going to fool around with that old tree, but if that's what you want, it's okay with me. Don't forget my editor is expecting me to send her my chapters this week. I won't have time to help if you need a second pair of hands. You do remember my deadline, don't you?"

"How could I forget?" By the time he showers and comes downstairs, sports coat over one shoulder, Millie is in the study, clacking away at her keyboard.

A few hours later, Thomas' silk sports coat lay heaped on the table in the Westfield Library. Here, two towns over from his home in Thurston, he feels safe. No one he knows comes here, especially during the day. The library is small, simply furnished with comfortable chairs, scuffed with use, but lovingly polished. He unpacks his laptop, pushes the case under his sports coat, fingers the gash where he'd cut out the Brooks Brothers label. Already, the threads are unraveling.

Wednesdays are Thomas's favorite day. Not because the workweek is mercifully coming to a close, but because this is the day he's assigned to observe the library program as part of the university course he's taking: *Introduction to Teaching for the Transitioning Professional.* He sits so his six foot two doesn't frighten the little people— some only knee high— gathering around the librarian, anxiously waiting for her to read. Her silvery hair is pulled back from her affable face in a chignon. Dressed like Mother Goose, in a bonnet with loose flowing ties, her full-length white apron falls in gentle folds around her ankles. A dark lad shyly fondles the fabric. No one seems to have cajoled him into coming here, and the little guy's not clamoring to be the biggest, the best. He is simply and fully here. With nothing to prove.

Thomas feels as if he's learning, as these children are, to become a human being, not a human doing. Sure, there's a certain amount of "doing" to his day, starting each morning with his Unemployed Exec meetings, a kind of twelve-step program where, a few hours earlier, he stood before a half dozen white guys confessing his resume writing efforts were halfhearted at best. Then networking with the other 'ex-ecs,' as they call themselves, looking on as they furiously studied Web-sites for postings of new "positions." Not jobs but positions. Not what he wants.

Afterward, while waiting for his appointment with his counselor, he looked forward to speaking openly with someone who was, until not long ago, a perfect stranger. Perfect in that he was doing exactly what he wanted, living exactly where and how he wanted, dropping *r*'s all over the place, braying his *a*'s and sounding unabashedly like a true and improper Bostonian. "Damn, I'm jealous," Thomas had told him. This long, skinny bearded fellow listened, his chin resting on his hairy knuckles, his unassuming shirt rumpled around his waist.

"What's stopping you, Thomas? Land a couple of interviews, use that jive. See how people respond."

But Thomas didn't want an interview. Sure, he'd finished his resume, he had to, it was part of his new program. But he used small font and listed his academic background last. No summa cum bullshit. Not anymore. He opens his notebook, turns on the computer, then stops to watch the robins flitting in and out of the cherry tree on the other side of the bay window. He envies their freedom, savoring his own, stolen though it may be. One of these days, he's going to have to tell Millie, and, as he told the long-legged counselor, that was his greatest fear.

"What do you think she'll do?" the counselor asked.

"I call her my blue-blooded black woman; she likes her work at the university, but loves the idea that she's doing it because she wants to, not because she has to."

"So you're worried she'll balk when she finds out you want a job teaching instead of a corporate position? What's the worst thing she would do?"

Thomas paused for a second, his eyes becoming filmy. "Know I'm a fraud."

He stares at his keyboard, until a woman's voice interrupts. "Having trouble with your laptop?"

Thomas' sports coat falls limp on the floor and in his rush to pick it up, he knocks his chair over. "You scared the sh …"

he starts to say, then seeing Mrs. Worthington's shocked face, "Sorry, you startled me." He rights the furniture, retrieves his jacket.

"I'm just as surprised to see you. What are you doing, research for your office?" With an amused smirk, she cranes her flaccid neck, peers at his notebook. Thomas reaches out, slams it shut. She raises her silvery eyebrows, and repositions her glasses with a swift movement like the one Grandma Betsy used to make. Thomas is astounded, entranced. But it's her attitude that gets to him. Aloof, withholding, judgmental. He wheezes, once, twice, feels the old humiliation washing down the back of his throat.

"How's Dr. Clark, that impressive wife of yours? I apologize, but I seem to have forgotten her first name. I was hoping she'd accept my invitation to join the Junior League. Diversity's our theme this year, and it would have been so..." An angry flash registers on Thomas' face, and her voice trails off.

"Millie. Her name's Millie," he says in a rush. "I don't know where she'd find the time. She's so busy. Writing a textbook, working on a grant, driving into Boston to teach..." He stops blathering, notices the Grand Dame of Thurston staring at his Franklin planner, at his ten-thirty counseling appointment, the only thing on the page. Thomas tosses his sports coat over the planner. He's thirteen years old again, incensed at his grandmother for checking his homework. "Not good enough," he recalls her saying. "Make it your best, nothing less than your best. Then I'll be proud."

Mrs. Worthington glowers, seems to understand he has a lot to hide. "My meeting's about to begin. Just think how delighted the regional board will be to hear that the financial community finds our little library so useful." Thomas says goodbye, folds his hands to stop them from shaking.

He isn't sure what makes him do it, but as Mrs. Worthington turns to leave, he shouts after her. "Why can't you be honest enough to ask what I'm doing here, with all these wonderful children?" Isn't she impressed that he's preparing for his future, in spite of what happened to him at Winston-Harding? Doesn't she know that other execs in his group are on heavy dosages of anti-depressants and he's doing okay? "Not one pill. Can you hear me, Mrs. Worthington, damn it?" he screams as she inches away from him.

The librarian corrals the terrified children and in a shaky singsong voice leads them out of the room with, "Let's pretend this is a fire drill, children. Who remembers which door we use?" Thomas slumps into his seat, head in his hands. Within minutes he's alone. An eerie silence floats through the library until it's broken by the distant wail of sirens.

Thomas takes the long way home, parks his car in the garage, places his briefcase in the foyer and listens for Millie's keyboard. He envies her focus and industriousness, even though it's fueled by fury. By now, Mrs. Worthington has called; he's sure of it. Millie's typing has that "if you think I believe you for an instant, you're an idiot" rhythm. She's right; he's an idiot and a liar.

The grandfather clock in the study chimes seven. Friday, August fifth is outlined in red on Millie's desk calendar. In less than three days her chapter's due. Millie's one of a team of researchers writing a medical textbook that promises to revolutionize doctors' training. Make it more holistic. Once it's published, Millie will be invited to lecture at med schools throughout the country, and Tufts will surely offer her the department chair. It's Millie's turn; her star's about to ascend. And leave him behind.

Thomas closes his eyes, rests his head against the doorjamb.

"You okay?" Millie asks, approaching him with cautious curiosity, one that maintains a respectful distance.

He stares down at her. She's a good six inches shorter than Thomas and half his weight. So, what is it about her that makes him quake? Perhaps it's her unwillingness to see that his high-powered position has made them wealthier and poorer at the same time. Left her thinking they deserved all they had. He can smell her sense of entitlement. A sense he no longer pretends to share.

He loosens his tie, unbuttons his white shirt and steps further from her. "I'm tired. Today was exhausting," he says, then sorry he's mentioned this, comes closer, pecks her cheek.

"I haven't made dinner."

"That's fine. I'm going to work in the garage for a while. I drew a sketch; nothing fancy, but I think you'll like it." Thomas opens his briefcase, hoping to distract her, and takes out a paper scratched with numbers and little arrows.

"A sketch of what?"

"The bench I'm going to make."

She rolls her head back, laughs. "So that's why you're home early. I figured you wouldn't get home before midnight—it's the second Wednesday of the first quarter—isn't this when you have your dinner meeting with the board?"

Thomas doesn't answer.

"Am I mumbling again?"

"I rescheduled the meeting to early morning, just for the summer months," he says, annoyed at the cute reminder she uses whenever he doesn't respond.

"Those Daddy Warbucks obsessing about the stock market?"

"With five percent unemployment, they can't help but worry," he says and starts up the stairs. Halfway up, he turns wondering if she's buying this line. "Can you help me...for just a few minutes?"

She glances at the study door, back at Thomas, her expression wooden. "Okay, but I won't have time to make dinner. You'll have to settle for sandwiches." Sandwiches. A feast as far as he's concerned.

By the time she changes into a pair of cut-offs and an old top, Thomas is in the third bay of the garage. His paint-spattered workbench runs the length of the outside wall, overflows with coffee cans and artichoke bottles filled with nails and screws. A spider has spun its web from the drill press to the leg of a chair wedged within a small vise. Scattered across the bench are cords, switches, stiff paint brushes.

Thomas' radial arm saw makes a whiny sound that becomes higher, more intense as the blade labors through a knot in the birch. His safety glasses dangle from a nearby nail and sawdust clings to the lenses like iron filings to a magnet. He gives the wood an extra push toward the blade, slicing the branch in two, letting it clatter to the floor.

When he turns around, Millie's reading the mail, scowling. "What's this about?" she says, handing him a letter from the bank. "The last time I looked at the accounts we had plenty of money. This can't be true—I'm mortified."

Mortified? That's nothing compared to how he felt after this afternoon's scuffle with Mrs. Worthington, Thurston's local broadcasting system. Thomas glances at the letter, clears sawdust from his throat. Sniffles. "That damn bank's always making mistakes—they've confused our account number with someone else's. I'm playing golf with the president tomorrow, I'll take care of this."

He takes the letter from Millie, stuffs it in his back pocket. "I don't know why they sent this here—I've asked them to send everything to my office. All our files are there." He gathers the logs, heaps them into her arms. "The two smaller pieces are for the arms, the others, the seat."

She stands, pressing the logs to her chest. "But all our checks are stamped 'insufficient funds.' This doesn't make sense."

Thomas turns towards his workbench and rattles through boxes, cans, wires. "Where'd I put that damn thing? Millie, can you see the paper with my notes?"

She squats, lowers her arms and drops the logs. She stacks them, the two longest together, the next size, then the next. She rests for a moment, her forearms on her thighs, wrists dangling from her knees, marionette-like. Exactly the way Thomas felt as a kid. Exactly how he feels now: taut, suspended by a woman. Always a woman.

Beginning with his grandmother, strong, tall as a mountain, someone who never missed an opportunity to remind him he was carrying the banner for the rest of his kind. Not wanting to disappoint, he earned a full scholarship to the University of Pennsylvania, then one to grad school at Wharton, and a fellowship at Oxford. Grandma Betsy had been right; it came naturally for Thomas, this ability to cash in on his gift. But somewhere along the way, it stopped feeling like his, seemed more a part of his grandmother's iron hand, the one that twitched beneath her velvety glove.

For a moment, Thomas can't bring himself to look at his wife, who flattered him into taking the position at Winston-Harding. Said being its youngest, smartest, first black chief financial officer was a coup. But it'd been a bitch.

"There's your sketch, by your foot," Millie says.

He glares at her. "You knew where it was all along—you made me look for it." He tosses a hammer that ricochets off the drill, clatters to the cement.

Millie jumps back. "For God's sake, Thomas, what's going on?"

Satisfied that he's blamed her for his chaos, he starts to drill, bearing down on the rotating bit, sinking deeper, deeper into a branch until it pops through the other side. "Shit!" he shouts, and throws the drill on the floor. "I ruined it. I was fine until you started asking questions. Now I can't concentrate. Shit!"

Millie's eyes narrow. "When did you move our files to your office?"

Thomas shifts his jaw from side to side, wheezes and takes a couple of deep breaths. "Remember when we first moved here?"

"Why?"

"I hated dragging you through that first black family in Thurston, the hidden jewel of the Berkshires crap. Being referred to as a family of color, as if we were part of some sociology prof's experiment. The champions of political correctness drew straws to see who would invite us to their home first. But after their leader, Mrs. Worthington, saw me walking toward her on Main Street, and tightened her grip on her purse, I knew I was a living lie."

Thomas stares at the ruined branch, hands on his hefty hips, shirt half unbuttoned. "She was amazed at your freckles, green eyes and credentials. Just think, a doctorate in occupational therapy, Grand Dame Worthington said. Imagine what she would have said if..." Thomas switched to his shoe shine boy accent, "I'd come out 'o my mama a deep dark molasses, a real colored boy, like my granddaddy."

"Has someone at work said something to you? That's discrimination, you know."

He shakes his head, points to the log by his tool chest. "Hand me that piece of wood. I pushed too hard. I'll be more careful this time."

His fingers circle a knot on the branch. Blackened and wrinkled, it reminds him of his scruffy elbows, when he was a boy. Beyond it, jagged scars intersect the whiteness of the bark, cut across the horizontal stitches that seem to fasten it to its tree.

Thomas asks Millie to hold the pieces in place while he screws them together. They repeat this until they've fastened the arms to either side of the seat and the legs beneath.

He steps back, studies his bench, runs his hand over the slight bow in the arms, thinks it artistic. But the arms seem, when compared to the legs, with their knobby knees and flat feet, too classy for this furniture. Clunky and amateurish are the words that come to mind. Not what he intended.

"I have work to do. Need anything else?" Millie asks.

"If you hold the back upright against the seat, I'll drive in the screws."

Millie places her feet shoulder width apart, and positions her small round hips as if she were about to lift a three hundred pound patient from his hospital bed. "Wood's wet, it'll get lighter when it dries out," he says, the bark bristly against his palms. Squatting beside her, Thomas holds the back in place with one hand, and drills with the other. With what he imagines to be the force of a powerful magnet, the boring screw draws the back from their grip, releases them from its awkward weight.

Millie tucks her hands into the pockets of her jeans, cocks her head to one side. "Reminds me of a newborn calf."

"Imagine that. All four feet actually touch the floor."

She puts one hand on each arm of the bench. "Dare I wiggle it?" He chews his lip and nods.

Not only does it wiggle, but it groans, one branch grinding against the other. Millie jerks around, as if to hide this mess from Thomas. He gasps, pulls his inhaler from his pocket, sticks it in his mouth and squirts.

"Guess I'm not as good as I thought. Something's got to change," he says with a growl. A trickle of salty liquid rolls down his throat and he knows he can't go on this way. What would Millie think if they sold this house and he took a job in Boston teaching poor white and black and tan kids? Math, perhaps. Self-respect, for sure. It has a certain appeal although he isn't sure he's what they call a role model. What's to respect about someone who lets others use screaming yellow highlighter to map out his life from one ivy tower to the next, from one influential cocktail party to the next charity fund raiser, where the folks in the we've-got-it-all crowd mill about, congratulating themselves on having lots to share?

"What do you have in mind?" Millie asks, her glasses dangling on a pearl chain that rests on her small breasts, peering into her heart.

"Remember when we used to play charades?"

"We haven't done that in ages. Getting sentimental, Thomas?"

"You haven't been doing that, but it's been different with me."

"I'm not following you. With this and lots of things."

"I'm not surprised." Thomas' heart is exploding, terrified by the truth he's about to spew.

"I'm thinking of donating this bench to the Salvation Army, taking it as a tax write-off." This notion entertains him, and he smiles until he sees the intensity on Millie's face.

"Hello? Earth to Thomas, this is your wife speaking. You're not making any sense. What's going on?" Her voice is brittle. Demanding.

"Mars to Millie, Mars to Millie, you mean to tell me you haven't noticed anything unusual?"

"Goddamn it. Thomas, you aren't having an affair, are you?" Her mouth twists into an agonized frown.

Thomas throws his head back, hoots with laughter, doubles over and slaps his haunches again and again. "Why didn't I think of that? Me? An affair? Hell, who would have me? The guy who specializes in wobbly benches." His hooting slips into uncontrollable, hysterical laughter. Tears run down his cheeks. He sucks air in and out, until it gets caught in the emptiness deep inside him, and he chokes and coughs. Coughs until he can't stop. He's on his knees now, one minute face down on the cement, the next, head up, gasping for air, any amount of air.

"Thomas, use your inhaler. Stand up so we can get it out of your pocket. I'm calling 911." Millie's full moon eyes protrude, nostrils umbrella as if she were trying to take in air enough for them both.

He shakes his head. No. Waves his hand—no 911. He hadn't counted on scaring her like this, figured what he had to tell her would be terrifying enough. He follows Millie's trembling directions, "Sit up. Squirt. Breathe in, gently now, one, two. Breathe out," and she counts and counts until he gets hold of himself. He can almost taste the relief.

He grabs her hand, kisses it. "Sorry, I'm so sorry," he says, and with that, pulls her towards him.

"Thomas, tell me what's happening." Millie tucks his fuzzy head beneath her chin, squeezes it, as if to keep it from exploding.

"This is the freest this black boy has ever been," he says.

And he does what he should have done long ago. Tells her what it felt like to be the most sought-after CFO the company had ever had: speaking engagements, pricey consultations, talk of becoming the next CEO. And from a lofty perch, a terrible fall. His humiliation. The degrading satellite office, colleagues' averted gazes, his severance and with it, the realization that he never truly belonged. He tells her he wants to recreate his life, shapes his words to sound as if this was all part of his plan. As if he were in charge.

"How could that be? You just rescheduled your board meeting." Millie sits on his bench, waits for its jittery swaying to stop, her jaw suspended, eyes unblinking, seemingly struggling not to let his words sweep her away. Seeing her vacant stare, he imagines her taking refuge on high ground, far, far from him. Begins to understand the impact of his subterfuge. No, of his lies.

He becomes aware of the bottom of his sneakers on the cool cement, arms lightly touching the thinning denim surrounding his outer thighs, diaphragm against his shirt, blood spurting through his heart and into the circumstance he created, forcing him, for the first time, to a new kind of pain. Someone else's. Many minutes pass. Silence.

With one incredulous blink Millie's consciousness reenters the room. Thomas imagines her returning after the storm, to the site where her home had once been, to find it swept away with only the foundation remaining. "A whole year?" are the words she whispers. "And you're telling me now when I'm so close to the end of my project? You waited a year, but you couldn't hang on a few more days? Are you trying to ruin me too, Thomas? Is that it? One goes, we both go?"

"I meant to tell..." He stops mid-lie. I never meant to tell her a thing, otherwise why the ruse? So elegant. So smart.

"You didn't think I would help you. Didn't trust me. It's as simple as that," Millie says, her beautiful face crinkled in disbelief.

Her tone shifts and in one frozen breath sends Thomas's thoughts skittering toward their kids, wondering about the yet unspoken: joint custody, visitation schedule, court-ordered family life. He decides, this very moment, if that's what's to happen, he won't bother with an attorney, doesn't want a thing. I've had the best of the best, your honor, he imagines saying. A grandmother who promoted me, a wife who supported me, a CEO who gave me the chance of a lifetime. All of them trusted me. Until I drilled too far, and tore through their tender limbs. He runs his tongue over his teeth, gums, the roof of his mouth, and recognizes it at last. Relief, profound and delicious.

These thoughts make him giddy and scare the shit out of him. From somewhere in his past, he hears Grandma Betsy's voice, chiding him for using language that's common. "Shh," he whispers.

Millie looks up at him as if he were speaking to her. "I didn't say anything."

"Take your time," he says in the soft drawl he hasn't used in years. He moves closer, extends his left hand. Perhaps Millie will reach out for it, touch it because it's his. He waits, floating on the delicacy of this moment. When she doesn't move, he draws his fingers along the graceful curve of the birch arm, and stubs his toe against the monstrous foot. Such a hideous creation. He starts to wheeze, but stops himself. He wipes his nose with his shirt, doesn't care if she sees him. It doesn't matter now.

Millie shifts and the bench quivers with what Thomas hopes is a signal for him to sit beside her. He peers anxiously into her small face, sees no welcoming glimmer, but decides to sit, uninvited. After all, he's spent a lifetime in places where he's not welcome. Squeezed against her warm haunches, he finds an odd comfort in the way the bench presses against his ribs. Reads it as the truth of their lives: they manage to fit together, even though they'd each be more comfortable alone. Millie squirms. In the precarious moments that follow, Thomas sways in a barely perceptible dance, adjusting and counter-adjusting his weight, while his bench wobbles and threatens to collapse.

BOUNMA SONG YOUG O'REILLY

William's parents reminded him there was a war going on and if that foreign woman, "Mrs. Vietcong," made an attempt to speak with him, he was to continue walking without saying a word or making eye contact. He was twelve at the time, and pretty much did what he was told, until the following year, when his leukemia went into an unexpected remission, and he met Toady Johnson, the best friend he would ever know.

By then, William's father had purchased most of the rolling corn fields surrounding Linden, California, and was systematically reducing them to tidy lots marked by split levels and ranches with flagstone patios. As part of his agreement with the town, his crews widened the road leading to Linden Junior High, and excavated for sidewalks. "So our children will have a safe place to walk or ride their bikes," the officials liked to say.

Within weeks, dirt had been piled in mounds along the edge of crab grass lawns, and staked boards ran parallel down the entire length of Cross Street, where William lived with his parents. Crews spread truckloads of gravel in readiness for William's father's churning truck to dump yards of cement that would, within a mere twenty-nine days, become hard and unchanging. When neighbors complained of dust from her husband's never-ending construction, William's mother reminded them that Bill Darby Construction, Inc. was working hard to build a community where they could raise their children without worrying about traffic, deteriorating schools, and the influx of Negroes, Puerto Ricans, and who knows what else.

Early that July, town officials called William's father to make sure the sidewalks would be done in time for the opening of school. "As part of the town's safety campaign," they reminded him. William asked Toady why those officials never worried when Mrs. Vietcong pedaled her bike along-side tractors, farm trucks, and cars spewing dark smoke. Toady tossed a Tootsie Roll in his mouth and said he figured her slanted eyes had something to do with it. "And the fact that the 'suits' don't remember what it's like to ride a bumpy road with their bicycle seats slapping their privates."

Whenever William's mother drove past Mrs. Vietcong's bicycle, she swerved her pink Studebaker as if the rusty old bike with a basket strapped to the rear fender was a Mac truck. "God knows where she's going with all that stuff," she muttered through a haze of cigarette smoke.

William peered out the passenger-side window at bottles jiggling in Mrs. Vietcong's basket, while January, his shepherd-collie, poked her graying nose out the window and sniffed. "How does she keep the bottles in there? When I tried to carry a bottle of milk in my bike basket, it bounced out and smashed," he said.

His mother lit another cigarette. "You know that awful smell that comes our way when the wind is just right?" she asked. William nodded, figuring she was off on another of her favorite gripes: the burnt smell from the factory across the river, where Toady's father worked. "It comes from Mrs. Vietcong's kitchen. I hear she makes her own medicines." She gripped the cigarette between her lips while shifting into second gear. "You'd think she was a witch or something."

William's brown eyes widened in his puffy face; it was the first time he'd heard his mother call Mrs. Vietcong a witch. That kind of talk made him nervous—it meant his mother was worse off than he was.

That afternoon, perched in the top of the willow tree in their side yard, William steadied his telescope against the scratchy bark. Mrs. Vietcong's garden wasn't an ordinary patch like the small square of tomatoes his mother had planted by their kitchen door, or his father's rose beds on either side of the front steps. Rectangles of leafy vegetables swayed next to rows of grass-like greens, and branches crawled with vines in Mrs. Vietcong's garden. "Tidy," William said, "as one of Grandma Darby's patchwork quilts."

"I've got to get her to sell me her land," his father had said. "Kids in Cornfield Hills are dying to have a rec center." His mother shot him a dirty look when he said the word "dying;" William's goofy parents thought he didn't know how lucky he was to be alive. Didn't know he'd had his ear plastered to the door when Dr. Farber said his remission was temporary, and the only thing left was to pray for a miracle. His father's ghost-white lips were drawn downward when he came into the waiting room. William's mother dabbed her eyes. She took his chubby hand in hers as if to anchor him to this world. During their ride home, silence surrounded them like a too-tight pair of jeans. William imagined getting home and sitting between his parents on the green flowered sofa, where they would give him the bad news. They never did. And that made William hopping mad.

Mrs. Vietcong came out of her house. Dressed in a dark shirt, pants, and a green and red turban, she reminded him of an ant carrying a small watermelon. She walked, face down, between the endless rows of dark green, silver, and purple plants. Once in a while, she'd reach into the leaves, and come up with a wrinkled vegetable or fruit, he wasn't sure which. The scene was so peaceful, he longed to be part of it.

The next day, he and Toady walked on the unfinished sidewalks, small black stones crunching beneath their high tops. They'd almost reached Mrs. Vietcong's when Toady dared William to measure the distance from her bottom step to the sidewalk-to-be. "My mother says her place violates the zoning ordinance because it's too close to the street." Toady's horn-rimmed glasses slid down his snubby nose, and stopped at the world's biggest pimple—Toady's first.

William looked up Cross Street at the green, white, and gray houses; all were occupied except one that still had its *SOLD!* sign hanging from the string of small colorful flags his father had tied across the front porch. Each sat back from the road on a large patchy lawn with a paved driveway that lead to an attached garage. By comparison, Mrs. Vietcong's faded green bungalow with its lopsided shed and pricker bush hedge looked out of place. William scratched the reddish brush that had grown back on his head after his chemo.

"What am I supposed to measure with? Do you see me carrying a ruler?" he mumbled through the gauze mask his mother insisted he wear.

Toady pointed to William's sneakers. "Your gun-boats run about twelve inches. Measure with them."

William hesitated. Other than the time he and Toady had delivered flyers for Toady's mother when she was running for town selectman, he'd never been on Mrs. Vietcong's property. "You coming?" he asked.

"Me keep guard, Kemo Sabe," Toady said in his deep-throated imitation of Tonto speaking to the Lone Ranger. William rolled his eyes, pretended his heart wasn't hitting grounders into his chest.

"Watch out for her bottom step, it's rotting, remember? It's not a problem for Mrs. V.—she's only seventy-five pounds, but a guy like you..." Toady pointed to William's stomach pressing against the old white shirt he kept buttoned all the way to the top. William sighed. He knew what Toady meant; at one hundred and sixty pounds, his own shirts didn't fit him anymore, and his father's were getting tight. His medications were making him fat.

William rolled his sleeves. He creased them with his finger; leftover starch made them feel cardboardy. When he finally looked up, Toady's new braces sparkled behind his smirk. William fumed. He put his hands on Toady's puny arms, and moved him out of his way. "Whistle if anyone comes," he said. Toady's bug eyes got buggier. If there was one thing William couldn't stand, it was Toady's calling him chopped chicken liver—especially when he wouldn't say it out loud.

William stepped onto a mound of dirt. Rusty brown sand trickled over the top of his high-tops, down his ankle, and into his socks. "You're leaving tracks, we'll never make a clean getaway," Toady said with a groan.

"Shh." William peeked around the bushes at Mrs. Vietcong's staircase. All he had to do was put one foot in front of the other until he made it to her porch. Then, he would turn and run. The muscles in his thighs and arms twitched. A mosquito landed on his knee. William slapped it bloody, spit on the palm of his hand, scrubbed until his leg hairs were twisted into knots, then wiped the guts on his cut offs. Now, he was ready.

He butted his right toe to his left heel, then reversed the process up the small incline to the porch. He was concentrating on counting, "One foot...two...three..." when Toady yelled, "Bolt man, she's coming!"

William's head shot up. Mrs. Vietcong appeared out of nowhere. Maybe his mother had been right—she was a witch. A miniature witch, only a head taller than his waist, with curious eyes, and quiet movements. "Be careful," she said.

"Run, Kemo Sabe!" Toady screamed. The wild crunching of Toady's feet along the gravel meant he was taking his own advice. William turned, ready to leap. He pivoted on his right foot, and was about to do the same with his left, when the rubber tip on his sneaker caught the bottom step. Mrs. Vietcong dropped her basket, and grabbed for him, but he pushed her away just before landing smack on her step.

White pain bolted from his elbow to his shoulder. He wiggled his arm in an attempt to free it, but couldn't. "Holy sh—," he stopped himself, just as his father did when his mother was in earshot. Without thinking, he swung his right arm over his head, and smashed the soft wood from around his upper arm.

Mrs. Vietcong was talking fast in a tinny language that came from a part of the world he'd only read about. William sat on the ground, cupping his elbow with his hand, his breath sucked tight into his chest. Tears clung to his auburn eyelashes. Mrs. Vietcong looked blurry. He yanked off his mask. "My friend told me you were raising fire ants under that step." And the minute it came out of his mouth, he realized how stupid he sounded. His face burned. He was going to kill Toady.

Mrs. Vietcong squatted, took a man's handkerchief from her pocket, and held it to his elbow. Within seconds, red seeped onto its brown and blue plaid. "Fire ants were hungry," she said, her little face crinkling into a smile. William watched the calm with which she folded the stained handkerchief in half. She motioned for him to hold the handkerchief in place. Mrs. Vietcong pointed toward the house. "Come," she said, her knees lifting her out of her squat.

William had to kneel first. When he felt steady enough, he placed his foot on the ground, and pushed himself up. He swayed for a few seconds, thought he might pass out. Mrs. Vietcong moved close. "I'm fine," he said.

She folded her hands and bowed her head. "May I touch you?" she asked. "I want to make sure nothing is damaged, okay?" When he didn't reply, she looked up at him from beneath her tissue paper bronze eyelids. "In my country, we ask permission before we touch another's body. Like bowing, it is a sign of respect."

"Yeah, okay," he mumbled.

She lifted his arm, a little at a time, her dark eyes darting from it to his face. Her fingers moved to his shoulder, across his collarbone, and back. "Any pain?" she asked.

"A little."

"Come with me, please," she said, and hopped over the damaged step.

William's parents' warning returned to him. Sure, the country was at war, but he wasn't, and yes, if he didn't get to know this woman, she'd always be a stranger. With this came a heady rush, and the realization that his parents had stopped making sense. He listened for his mother's Studebaker, in case she was rumbling by, and when he was certain she wasn't, followed Mrs. Vietcong.

She stepped out of her flip-flops. It was a scene straight from *National Geographic.* He bent to untie his sneakers. "No need to do that. Come," she said, opening the door.

A menthol smell, like the stuff his mother used to rub on his chest, was the first thing he noticed. The sunny living room reminded him of the one at his grandmother's cottage at Lake Agatha: small and square with a couch with canoe-paddle arms. Beside it, a double-tiered table and a chipped lamp shaped like a horse's head. Mrs. Vietcong pulled the chain. A soft glow shone on an eight by ten photo of a serious looking man in an Army uniform. An American flag folded in a triangle rested beside it.

It occurred to William that her name wasn't Vietcong. Weren't they the bad guys the US was fighting in Vietnam? Weren't they the reason the local football hero, Bobby Phelps, never came home? Wasn't that why Bobby's parents hadn't yet moved into the house they'd bought on Cross Street? "Wracked with grief," his mother had said. Somehow, between trips to and from the hospital, and the hours he'd spent alone in his room reading *National Geographic,* slipping bits of paper to mark pages with the bare-chested women Toady wanted to see, he'd never thought to ask his parents why, when they said her name, they snickered. But the affect rolled in on him, quiet and unnoticed, like soggy air, dulling a penny's once flawless shine.

She took a few things from a brightly painted cabinet and put them on a tray. Her bare feet padded across the yellow linoleum. "This is gonna sound weird, but we've been neighbors for two and a half years, and I don't know your name."

"When I was a little girl in Laos, my parents called me Bounma Song. After they were killed, a missionary doctor from Vietnam adopted me and added Youg to my name. He and his wife sent me to school in Germany, where I met my husband, and became Bounma Song Youg O'Reilly."

"So rhythmic," he said, blushing. He shifted from a broken spring to the next cushion. He'd expected Mrs. Vietcong to have an accent, like the oriental guy who ran the laundry in the Saturday afternoon westerns he and Toady liked to watch. But she was Mrs. O'Reilly now, and that's how she sounded.

She pulled the cork out of a bottle, and poured dark liquid onto a piece of gauze. It added a newer, stronger smell to the room. She dabbed the gauze on his elbow. William winced. "This will clean your wound, and help it heal." She leaned toward the back of his arm. "You have a bad cut. I'll need to get something stronger—an ointment." She touched the mask hanging around his neck. "You probably aren't supposed to come in contact with germs."

"My mom makes me wear this, even though I'm in remission."

"Leukemia?" She seemed at home with his disease. He nodded. "I'm sorry," she said.

She'd drifted to a faraway place, where William suspected she'd learned more about suffering than he had, or would. William felt horrible for her. "Thanks, but I'm okay. Really. I'll be starting my freshman year at Linden High this fall. I'm in college prep. I plan to make honor roll, graduate as valedictorian, and go on to college, then med school." He stopped, not knowing who he was trying to convince—Mrs. O'Reilly or himself. "But, how did you know, Mrs. O'Reilly?"

"Dr. O'Reilly."

"You're a doctor? That's not what I've heard."

"People say what they want to believe, even though it may not be true."

"I've never seen you at the hospital, and I've been there a lot."

She looked sad again, only this time a different kind of sadness. "My medical training isn't recognized in the United States, so I can't work here as a doctor." She glanced at her dead husband's picture. "That's not why I'm here."

The only thing William knew about licenses was that every dog was supposed to have one, and he was sure that that didn't have much to do with her. "My father bought land from a farmer named O'Reilly."

"That was my husband's father. This is what is left of his family's farm. My husband convinced me to leave my work in

Vietnam, and come to a safe place. Now, I try to help people like myself who were forced to leave their homes..."

"Those bottles in your bike basket—are they for them?" William asked.

She tilted her head and smiled. "You are an observant young man. You'll make a good doctor."

So she knew. She'd probably seen him spying on her from his tree. He felt foolish and embarrassed. Toady's whistle saved him. "I better get going." He hurried to the door. "My arm feels better. Thanks, Dr. O'Reilly." He slipped his mask up over his nose.

"You're welcome, Kemo Sabe."

William smiled. "That's a joke between my friend and me, because of this." He pointed to his mask. "My name's William." Toady whistled again, this time louder, more demanding.

"I haven't given you your ointment, William."

"Thanks, but I've got to go." He stepped over Dr. O'Reilly's flip-flops, down two steps and over the one he'd broken. He felt like he did a few weeks ago when he'd ridden his bike over the cliff at the sand quarry: shaken, bruised, thrilled to be alive, and determined to do it again.

Toady stood on the other side of Dr. O'Reilly's pricker bushes, his thumb and index finger pressed to his lower lip, ready to let out his all-alert whistle. "Five more minutes and I was going to call the cops," Toady said. He looked at his friend's arm—at the house and back at the arm. His eyes narrowed with suspicion. "Tell all."

They walked toward home, their mouths filled with Tootsie Rolls. "She's nice—and she's not a witch." He swallowed, and went on to tell Toady how her husband had died in Vietnam, and that she was a doctor in her country.

"And which one is that?" Toady asked.

William knew what he was asking; Bobby Phelps' mother had started the rumor that Dr. O'Reilly was a communist, and named her Mrs. Vietcong. "I'm not sure," he fibbed. While Dr. O'Reilly had been describing the pain of leaving her home, knowing she'd never again see the familiar faces or breathe the sweet night smells, she bumped into the worries that haunted him. Special worries he wasn't ready to share with Toady.

"If she's a real doctor, how come you're the only one who knows?" Toady asked.

Dr. O'Reilly's words about people saying what they wanted to believe ran through William's mind. He could continue teasing Toady with tidbits of information that would make his short arms fly in the air, and his face turn red from screaming. As temping as it was to drive him into a frenzy, William stopped. He'd never kept secrets from Toady, until now.

Later, alone on his back porch, William thought about this afternoon as he stared at the hibiscus hedge. Its leafy branches bowed to touch the ground, making its leafy tunnels one of the best hiding places in Cornfield Hills.

While he waited for his mother to call, "Bill...William...dinner," he studied the bottom step. It looked pretty simple, actually. A few boards nailed tight against one another. From what he could see, there were two problems: getting hold of the wood, then cutting it to size. No, there was one more: fixing Dr. O'Reilly's step without Toady finding out.

Toady had already begun teasing him about having been alone with Dr. O'Reilly. "What was it like having inscrutable oriental nurse your wound?' Toady asked, combining a hokey oriental accent with that awful leer he made when he thumbed through his *National Geographics.* Sometimes he could be so weird!

"It was like being in Dr. Farber's office, without the needles," William said, even though it wasn't like that at all. Dr. Farber was tall and starched as his white lab coat, distant and cold as the moon. When William told him he wanted to become a doctor, the creep gave his mother and father a weird look—as though he knew his wish would never come true.

Friday nights, William's mother made franks and baked beans, William's favorite. Seated opposite his father at their yellow Formica table, William was about to put a piece of hotdog in his mouth when his mother cleared her throat. He took his fork out of his mouth and looked at her. She was busy cutting her hotdog into bite-sized pieces. She glanced at him and cleared her throat again. What had he done wrong, he wondered? He had yet to drink from his glass of milk, so there were no telltale signs of "washing his meal down." And he'd cut his hotdog with his knife, instead of spearing it, and chomping off the end. William pulled his chair closer to the table. His mother took her paper napkin from her lap and dabbed at the pink lipstick on her thin lips. Then she glared at his napkin, still folded in a perfect triangle to the left of his plate. "Oh," he said, reaching over his plate with his right hand and whisking it off the table. Ever since that day in Dr. Farber's office, his mother had treated him like a thin-shelled egg. It left him feeling scrambled.

His mother turned to his father. "How was your day, dear?"

His father snorted. "Tough. My lawyer wants to see what we can do about getting that woman up the street to sell her land. Looks like it's going to take a while." He sighed. "I asked him to speed it up so I can excavate this fall."

William stopped chewing. His father was talking about Dr. O'Reilly. About his plan to build a pool and a recreation center on her property. William thought he'd given up on that idea. He sat up straight and leaned forward, then slouched; he didn't want to seem too interested.

"Lawyer talked about something called eminent domain." His father's fork clicked against his plate as he speared a chunk of hotdog.

"I don't get it, Dad. What's eminent domain?"

His father's sunburned face relaxed into a smile, as if seeing his son for the first time today. "Under certain conditions, the state can take a person's property."

"Without their permission?"

His raised his brown eyebrows and nodded. "That's right."

"But this isn't the USSR. It's a free country. The government can't just take something that belongs to you." William's voice was getting louder. He was afraid something terribly wrong was about to happen, and that his father would be the cause of it. He hadn't felt this kind of anger since he'd begged his father to tell him what it meant for a ten-year-old boy to have leukemia. Even then, his father hadn't told all.

"It doesn't work that way," his father said. "The government can only take private property if the common good is at stake."

"I still don't get it."

"If the town of Linden needed to have a safe place for the kids in town to 'hang out' as you say, and the only available location was Mrs. Vietcong's land, they could offer to buy it. If she refused to sell, they could go to court to prove that a rec center is necessary for public safety. If the court agreed, it would give the town permission to take her land from her."

"But what if that's all she has?" William blurted, annoyed at this and his father's calling Dr. O'Reilly, Mrs. Vietcong.

"Sweetheart, you sound upset. Are you feeling okay?" His mother reached out for his arm. He pressed his elbow to his side.

"I am kind of tired. I'm going to lie down for a bit," William fibbed. His head whirled. Dr. O'Reilly had lost her family, her husband, her job, and now her home?

His mother's gray-brown eyes scanned his face, then his empty plate. "I worry about the way you and Toady disappear for hours at a time. You're not supposed to overdo, remember? The doctor said you should take a nap every afternoon."

"I'm not overdoing it, Mom. Toady and I aren't always running around. We hang around a lot and rest. Honest."

He could tell his mother didn't believe him, but didn't want to get into it. Didn't want to get herself riled up. The doctor said he'd live an "almost" normal life; for a while, that is. She sighed, pulling her lips into her "just think about getting better" expression, the one she'd put on each time he peered at her through the jail rails of his hospital bed.

January's nails clicked against the kitchen floor as she pushed herself up. She straightened each of her front legs slowly, grunting as she did. "Arthritis." That's what his mother had called her ailment. "Lots of old dogs get it. There's nothing we can do."

This was her classic non-explanation. At least his father understood how things worked. Even though William didn't like what he was planning to do to Dr. O'Reilly, he'd take his brand of rock solid reasoning any day over the way his mother shrugged her shoulders and went along or, worse yet, repeated things that weren't true.

He lifted January and carried her up the stairs. When she was little, he'd bury his head in her shinny black coat and breathe her sweet puppy breath. Now she was fat, like him. Her coat had grown coarse, and her breath foul. His mother had warned him that January wouldn't be around forever. The thought of losing her terrified him. He tightened his arms around her.

With his bedroom door closed behind him, he spread his legs the width of his hips, and tried lowering himself into a squat, like Dr. O'Reilly had done. He pushed his rump down so his knees would get close to his ears, and almost lost his balance. He caught himself before landing on his sore elbow. "I hate being this fat," he muttered.

William unbuttoned his shirt and scowled at his flabby breasts. He craned his neck to check his elbow. The back of his arm glistened blue-black. A light scab had formed over his elbow, and the bandage on the back of his arm was damp. He yanked it off. The cut oozed. He patted the area with the pads of his fingers, the way Dr. O'Reilly had done. His skin was pink and hot. William imagined it growling at him, the way January did when Toady tried to take her bone from her. He got a bandage from the medicine chest in the bathroom. Dr. O'Reilly was right. An infection was the last thing he wanted, especially when he had so much work to do.

With ruler in hand, he reached down to his sneakers. Toady was right—his feet were twelve inches exactly. He did a few calculations, and fixed the decimal point in the right spot. When he finished, he leaned back, checked his math, and slipped the paper into his pocket for later that evening.

William lay beneath the sheets in his cut-offs and pajama tops. He wished he could sleep with his back to the door as he usually did, but the weight on his arm was painful. He tented his right hand over his throbbing elbow.

His mother came in, kissed him lightly on the forehead. "Mummy loves you," she whispered. She tugged on the top sheet, straightening, then tucking it in. "Hmm," William groaned, and turned his head away from her. "Night, baby," she said, and tiptoed out of the room.

He could see his parents' light lining the gap beneath his door. He waited for it to disappear, then waited a while longer. The house settled into its night sounds: the purr of the refrigerator, a muffled crack of the foundation settling, the drip of the bathroom faucet, the hum of a fan. William opened his bedroom door, and listened for his parents' stirring in the room across the hall. Other than his father's raspy snores, followed by his mother's soft puffs, there was none.

William reached under the bed for his sneakers and the fresh pair of socks he'd placed beside them. He tried Dr. O'Reilly's straight-backed squat once again. Between his tight hamstrings and a stomach lumpy as cottage cheese, it was no wonder he couldn't make it. But that would soon change. That afternoon, he'd fed January the plateful of cookies his mother baked for him each day. More importantly, he'd taken the medicine she'd placed beside it, and flushed it down the toilet.

He plunked his butt on the floor. January lifted her head in sleepy curiosity. "No noise," William whispered in her ear. "You stay here. That way, if Mom comes in the room, she won't think I'm gone. Got that?" The light from the street lamp shone on January's wet nose. William took the extra pillows from his closet, and shaped them as if he were sleeping on his side. He pulled the covers over his goose feather head. Now, he was ready.

Outside, the air was thick and still. William listened for animals. A raccoon, a 'possum, perhaps a deer. Nothing. The thrill of being up while others were stumbling through their dreams thrilled him. For the first time since he stopped being a boy and became a diagnosis, he'd taken charge of his life.

He tucked his pajama top into his cut-offs, and headed to the far end of the street, where Bobby Phelps' house stood empty. The farther he walked, the fewer the streetlights. Soon, the glow from the one by his house seemed like a distant star.

He imagined himself on another planet, the lone explorer, adventurer and scientist extraordinaire, there for the sole purpose of finding a cure for leukemia. "My investigations," he'd told his colleagues at the university center back home, "have lead me to believe that a microscopic nugget, found only in the rock formations on Nebdula Major, light years from earth, hold the key to this disease."

"But Dr. Darby," they'd argued, "You're too valuable a scientist to undertake this journey. What if something happened to you? What would become of our research?" He scratched his shocking red beard. What to tell them? He picked up a couple of pebbles, slipped them in his pocket. "Get to work," he said aloud. He had to stop fooling around.

Something rustled in the bushes. William jumped. "Oh, my God!" he said, slapping his hand to his chest as a critter scampered off into the woods. He tiptoed across the street, his heart beating hard and fast. From beneath a log by the side of the road, he pulled out the crowbar he'd hidden, and ran to the other side of the street where wild animals wouldn't dare go.

Dead weight; that's how the crowbar felt hanging from his fist. Eventually, if he kept holding it this way, it would tear his arm out of its socket, and his father would want to know what he'd been doing with his crowbar. Then he'd have to tell him. He wished he already had. How would he punish him? Ground him for disobeying his mother? Big deal. That was nothing compared to what his father would do if he found out that he was about to undo the work he'd paid his crews overtime to complete.

Tanned, sweaty and strong. William had watched his father's men stretch a mason's grade from stake to stake to establish grade for the sidewalk. Later, they'd use double-headed nails to attach two by fours to the stakes. It was the two by fours William wanted.

Dr. O'Reilly's bottom step was about twelve by thirty-six. He wouldn't have to deal with a baluster since her railing ended on a cement slab on the ground. He thought about how neat it was to know terms like baluster and mason's grade. If he'd learned those by just hearing his father talk about them, he should have no difficulty learning about the human body and how it worked. Just like Dr. O'Reilly.

He dug in his pocket for his calculations. With his flashlight shining on his square block letters, *Restoration Project: 235 Cross Street* seemed very professional. He'd circled the goal for tonight: unstake four point two five boards. He'd have to get five.

With the curve of the crowbar pressed to the ground, he slipped the forked end around the double-headed nail. His father always said that double head nails were expensive, but he made up the cost on labor when it came time for his men to remove the forms. "The quickest part of the job," he'd called it. And he was right. All William had to do was lean on the crowbar and the nail squealed out.

Every thirty inches, there was a stake. William worked quickly, squatting in his awkward way, removing the nail, and pocketing it, then getting up, and moving his equipment to the next nail. He stopped for a second to figure it out. Five, six foot boards equaled three hundred sixty inches divided by thirty. Twelve stakes—he needed twelve nails in his pocket.

Using the crowbar as a lever, he wedged it under the first board, then pushed down against gravel. Its crunching sound reminded him of Cocoa Puffs, which made him wish he hadn't fed his mother's oatmeal cookies to January. The board hardly budged. He crab-walked a few inches, and repeated the process. By the time he'd done this along the length of the board, it was lose enough to lift. The board made a sucking noise, like the awful sound of a tooth being pulled.

Everything took longer than he'd expected. William managed to free four boards. He hadn't counted on them being so awkward to carry, and wondered if he should get his Red Flyer wagon. But that would take more time. He worried that his mother might get up to use the bathroom, and on her way back to bed, check on him. When he thought of her curlered head peeking into his room, seeing his pillow form with January on the floor beside his bed, he relaxed. He'd thought of everything. Everything except his fatigue.

Seated on the edge of the last board, he flicked off his flashlight. "No use wasting the batteries," he said in a soft voice. He repeated himself, this time in his regular voice—but it had become cracked and gravelly. He recited his favorite part of the Lone Ranger's Creed: "*I believe that all things change but truth...and that truth alone lives on forever.*" His voice refused to come; it never did when he was tired. He hooked the crowbar on his belt, jammed the flashlight in his back pocket, and stooped to lift four boards. He was one short, like everything else in his life. He had no choice—he'd have to come back for the last one later, when he felt better.

At eight o'clock the next morning, the coffeepot was perking in its usual steady rhythm when the phone rang. Toady's mother. From what William could make out, Bobby Phelps' body would be arriving at the airfield in Los Angeles that evening. He stopped thinking about the boards he'd stashed under the hibiscus and listened.

"No thanks, you don't have to pick me up, Bill will want to go, I'm sure," William's mother said.

As she hung up the coffee's perking became fierce, hitting what she referred to as its "crescendo." His mother twirled *Tang* into a glass of water, wiping her tears with her shoulder. William put his arms around her waist. He wished Bobby hadn't died. He didn't want anyone else to die because every time they did, it made his mother think of what was going to happen to him. "Gee, Mom, don't stir mine too much, okay?" he asked. He liked to scrape the tiny granules from the side of the glass, and suck them off the spoon. "I almost forgot," she said, and kissed the top of his head.

The phone rang again. Toady's mother saying the funeral would be tomorrow at St. James' Episcopal Church. Nine o'clock. "We'll be there. Definitely. Black linen and my matching hat," William's mother said.

His father came into the kitchen. Small tears of blood-dotted toilet tissue were stuck like soiled snowflakes on his chin. "Damn Vietcong began another offensive. Wiped out an entire platoon," he said. "I got so disgusted, I wanted to toss Tom Jenkins and his radio show out the window." He poured himself a mug of coffee and sat down. William and his mother glanced at one another.

"Bobby Phelps is coming home today," his mother said. She let the weight of the words settle in the room. "Remember when we all lived in Los Angeles? Bobby used to bring

William to the playground and push him on the swings. He was always so careful with William." Her eyes welled.

William's Dad plunked his mug on the table, made the butter knife jump off its dish. "I'm going to miss that kid. He was one of my best summer workers." The phone rang.

Without looking, his father reached his long arm behind him, and picked up the black receiver. "Crankshaft's shot? That's what I suspected. You're kidding, next week? You're going to put me out of business—I've got three miles of sidewalks to pour. The cement has got to cure before school opens and that's in…" He opened the closet door, and ran his finger along the calendar pinned to the inside. "…six weeks. That's cutting it close. Can't you do better than that? Yeah. Okay, Sammy, let me know. Thanks."

At the mention of sidewalks, William slouched in his seat. At first, he'd been grateful for Sammy's call; at least his father wasn't talking about being dead or dying, although the topic of sidewalks was almost as bad. His head ached and arm throbbed. Before coming downstairs this morning, he'd pinched his cheeks so he wouldn't look so pale. Maybe he'd sneak over to Dr. O'Reilly's, and ask her to take a look at his arm.

Other than the clinking of William's spoon at the bottom of his bowl of Cocoa Puffs, the kitchen was quiet. His father chewed on toasted Wonder Bread, his mother, Hollywood Rye, some new low-calorie bread. The phone rang, this time louder and sharper than before. William jumped.

"Ah, for Christ's sake," his father said into the phone. Bits of bread scattered with his words.

William's mother scowled. She'd asked his father not to bring that that kind of talk into her house.

"Get a couple guys and replace the damn boards. Cement delivery is going to be delayed as it is, and I don't need those idiots from public works calling it an attractive nuisance." He slammed the phone down.

"I've got to get to the office. Seems some kids stole part of the sidewalk. What else could go wrong today?" He bent and kissed the auburn curls his wife hadn't yet combed out.

He pointed to William and winked. "Be good," he said.

Perhaps visiting Dr. O'Reilly's fell outside of what his father meant by "be good," but as soon as his mother went upstairs to get dressed—a process that always took an hour—William knocked on Dr. O'Reilly's back door. A pungent odor wafted out her kitchen window. William knocked again, and waited. Just as he was about to leave, she appeared. Her dark hair was matted on one side and loose on the other, as if she'd just gotten up. Her eyebrows formed a line across her forehead. He'd never seen her scowl before, and it disappointed him. She'd been the only person, other than Toady, who seemed to know how to be happy. Something selfish in him didn't want that to change.

She brought her hands together at her waist as if she was praying, and bowed her head. William knew from his reading that hands held at head height meant the person being greeted was held in the highest regard. He put his palms together at his chest and returned her bow. "Did I wake you up, Dr?"

"No, a call from the husband of an old Laotian woman woke me at three o'clock this morning." She opened the door, and gestured for him to come in. His eyes caught the row of tiny jars filled with a dark piece of bark on the shelf above her stove.

"We've been getting calls all morning, too."

"I'm making my friend more medicine." She lifted the lid on a sorry old pot and stirred the bubbling yellow liquid. William put his hand to his nose.

"Where is your mask? Your mother won't be happy if she sees you without it."

"That's not the only thing she won't be happy about." Dr. O'Reilly looked puzzled. William rolled up his sleeve and showed her his arm. "I think it's infected," he said.

Dr. O'Reilly washed her hands. She pulled his bandage off quickly and with it, a bunch of reddish hairs. William winced, but didn't make a sound; this wasn't the worst pain he'd ever known; nothing could match the non-stop dry heaves that sent convulsions through his body after his last chemotherapy. She led him to the kitchen door and checked his arm in the light. "You've diagnosed it correctly. You will make a good doctor someday."

"I'm not supposed to get infections," he said. "Besides, my mother is going to get hysterical when she finds out what I've done."

"Why? It was an accident." Dr. O'Reilly motioned for him to follow her into the living room. The cabinet door clicked open. She removed two bottles, a jar, and some bandages, and put them on her tray.

"Because when you have leukemia, everything is about being sick."

"Your mother is right to worry. I'm going to clean that wound, and put an antibacterial ointment on it. Have your doctor check your blood count, just to be sure." He liked that she just said what she had to say, without hiding the truth. He winced when she patted his arm with a damp gauze. "Excuse me for a moment." She stopped, went into the kitchen, and lowered the heat on the stove. Before returning, she washed her hands.

The greenish ointment felt cool against his hot skin. Dr. O'Reilly made a bandage out of gauze, and fastened it with strips of flesh-colored tape.

"Did you make these medicines yourself?" William asked.

"I practiced medicine in the hills of Phongsali, with shamans and herbalists. There aren't many doctors in those parts, and no pharmacies. But we do have many of the plants your pharmaceutical companies make medicines from. So, I learned to make my own."

"There's a pharmacy in Linden. Why are you brewing..." He hadn't meant to use that word; it reminded him of his mother's meanness.

"Because my people don't like your doctors, and if they did, they wouldn't have enough money to buy their medicines." There was a weariness in her voice he hadn't noticed before.

"Do you think you'll go back to your country someday?"

She turned toward the living room. "This was my husband's home. I feel closest to him here. This is where I need to be."

Relieved she intended to stay, William wished she could be his doctor. "Have you ever taken care of a boy with leukemia?"

"The children who came to see me had parasites, malaria, or dysentery."

"Have you ever spoken to a boy who was dying?"

"Many times," she said without a flinch, just like he'd hoped.

"What did you tell him?" William found her eyes, and held them in his.

"I told him 'dying doesn't hurt, and when your time comes, the light from your spirit will become a star in the night sky from where you will be able to look down at me.' And before he did die, I asked him to send down his blessing."

"And what did he say?"

She glanced at her husband's picture. "He promised he would. And he has."

William shook his head in disappointment. He'd expected her to say something more scientific or more Buddhist perhaps. "That sounds like what you'd tell a little kid."

She smiled. "That was what I told my husband. And each night when the sky is clear, I look for the brightest star, and tell myself he's thinking of me."

"Do you think Bobby Phelps is there, too?" He wasn't sure she knew who Bobby was, and wasn't sure it mattered.

"Oh, yes. I'm sure of it."

A long, slow whistle came from beneath the window. William hoped she hadn't heard. "Sounds as if your friend wants you," she said. "Don't forget to have your doctor check your blood count."

William nodded. "Thanks, Dr. O'Reilly."

"Didn't get enough of her yesterday, huh?" Toady said as they walked towards Bobby Phelps' parents' vacant house.

"My arm hurts, I asked her to look at it."

Toady turned his head to see. "Ah, fresh bandages for the walking wounded, I see."

William scowled. He didn't want to talk about her. "You going to the airport this afternoon?"

"My parents are going. I have to stay home with the intruder." Toady's name for his two-year-old sister still made William smile. "You going?"

"Naw, I've got stuff I've got to do."

"Like what?"

It crept up out of nowhere, this urge to tell his best friend what he'd been up to. He glanced at Toady, trying to decide if he was the same friend who'd sworn an oath with him to live by the Lone Ranger's Creed...*to have a friend, a man had to be one.* His eyes bulged large and honest as ever. Toady had never said a word about the quarry, or the time William had bucked his mother's car all the way down the street until it finally stalled. He'd trusted this guy so much, he'd even told him he knew he was going to die. Soon.

"You promise not to tell?"

"Course not, you jerk." Toady glared at him. "What gives?"

William showed Toady the wood he'd stashed. Told him his father was going after Dr. O'Reilly's land. Breathing came easier now. So easy that he told him he'd stopped taking his meds.

"You sure you know what you're doing?" Toady asked. A glint of panic flashed in his eyes.

"Look at me." William spun around. "Do I look different?"

"Well, no, but…"

"But what?"

"You sound different. You're making me nervous, William. Bobby Phelps is the last neighborhood kid I want to see in a box, if you don't mind."

William didn't mind, he just didn't think Toady would be that lucky.

That evening, the headline beside the Bobby Phelps story in the local section of the Linden Times read *War Protestors Destroy Dead Soldier's Home Along With School Sidewalk.* "Good grief," muttered William. So that's why his parents had been in a tear all day. Men in suits with straw hats talked in hushed tones to his father, who kept on taking his baseball cap off, scratching his head, and putting it on.

"Who would do something like this?" his mother asked.

"Lillian, it's only four boards and a few broken windows. Let's not make a big thing out of this, okay? Connecting a little vandalism to an antiwar demonstration is a hell of a stretch."

"It's not the boards, Bill, it's the fact that this is exactly why we moved here. Don't you understand what this means?"

His father raised his eyebrows—a sure sign his patience was running low. "What does it mean?"

"It means things are changing, again. Changing, changing, changing. We've borrowed against everything we own to build this perfect little community and what happens? The riff-raff follows us. This is awful, Bill. Just awful." Other than the times he'd been in the hospital, he'd never seen his mother this upset. Almost hysterical.

His plan had been stupid. He hadn't imagined that a few missing boards would create such a bother. If his father's men hadn't replaced the boards, he would have sneaked out tonight, and pounded them back into place. What a fool he'd been. He could have saved his money, and paid someone to repair Dr. O'Reilly's step. Someone who knew what he was doing. All William knew now was that he was tired, really, really tired.

January snored beside him. The house was still. He must have fallen asleep. William looked out his window. The detectives' cars were gone, and so was his father's. He checked the time: six forty-five. Bobby Phelps was almost home.

William dangled his feet off the end of his bed. January licked his neck. "Ready for another romp, old girl?" Her thick tail thumped the wall. "Let's go."

His bike rested on its kickstand in the back of the garage. The cement floor gave off a cool, damp odor. William lifted the door. Guiding its rumbling weight up over his head made him feel stronger than he'd felt in a long time. Flushing his pills had been the right thing to do. January watched him lower the door, and followed him on his bike.

The wind in his face made William feel like eight years old again, that healthy time when his mother didn't spend hours gossiping, and his father was content to live in a city that someone else created. It'd been so different having parents who believed their son would grow up.

William had no idea what it would be like not to exist. Would he recognize his last breath when it came, he wondered? Would it burn like the vodka he and Toady had stolen from the bottle in his father's liquor cabinet? That night at the quarry, he and Toady read poems aloud, slurring the words, and raising jelly jars of vodka each time the poet mentioned death. William had seen a dead person once. Grandma Darby. Rosy lipped and peaceful, her waxy hands folded around her rosary beads. He'd stared at her polka-dot bosom in case she was just pretending to sleep. His mother said she'd "passed over" or was it "passed on?" What was the difference, he wondered?

One afternoon on his bed, he laid back, his arms across his chest, his mother's mirror by his side. On the count of three, he grabbed the mirror and held it above his head. With one eye open a slit, he watched himself playing dead. He imagined the softness of the satin pillow beneath his head, and the cloudy shadow from the lid of his casket.

Now that they were on the quarry road, January's nails had stopped making that clicking noise. And he had stopped riding. The hard ground had turned to sand, which sucked his wheels into a dry heave. The bike tipped. His feet sunk into sand. He leaned into the handlebars and pushed his bike forward. Once the ground turned hard again, he rode past the scruffy bushes to the edge of the cliff, and braked.

January stood by his front wheel, panting. William pulled a Thermos and rope from his saddlebag. "Here's some water, girl," he said, as he filled a small aluminum cup. January lapped noisily, then lay down. Mosquitoes swarmed. Flies buzzed. Catbirds sang. The sun dipped behind the pine trees on the ridge.

With his hands on his hips, William searched the quarry. The day's heat rose from the sand. He checked his watch. Bobby Phelps' body would be arriving at the funeral home just about now. He took a deep, jagged breath. He didn't want to think about dying, although tonight he planned to honor the one who'd taught him how to do it: Bobby Phelps.

The memory of a scent as breathtaking as a young man's sweat—Bobby's, perhaps—filled Williams nostrils. Just like the night Bobby had stood beside him, pointing. "See that spot in the middle? That's where you aim your front tire," he'd said.

"What if I don't make it that far?" William asked.

"Don't worry, man, you will." Bobby backed his bike up to the place where the sand turned to ledge, raised the pedal up, and pounced on it with all his weight. William had never seen him ride that fast—faster than the wind. Past William, onward toward the ledge and... William sucked his eyelids into his skull. "Oh shit!" he yelled, as Bobby scrunched down behind his handlebars, and disappeared over the cliff.

"He-aah," Bobby screamed.

For an awful second, there was no sound until William heard the thud of bike parts against sand. He rushed to see. From the center of the pit, Bobby waved his flashlight—his signal that he was all right. William's breath rushed from his chest. The muscles at the sides of his mouth pushed into a tight-lipped smile, and William started breathing regular again.

It took Bobby a while to drag his bike up the side of the quarry, and the first thing he said when he saw William's worried expression was, "Don't worry about dying man, go for the gusto."

William cupped his hands around his mouth and yelled, "I tried, Bobby. I tried my best." Now it was his turn. An upside down bowl of darkness was closing in on him. A faint ridge of sunlight lingered behind the trees.

"I'm going to tie you here, okay?" January looked at him through the filmy clouds swallowing her eyes. She whimpered as she tried to push herself up from alongside the cliff. "Wait, I'll help you." William straightened his back and squatted.

"January, I did it," he said, his knees close to his ears. January cried again. William collapsed his knees to one side to get up and as he did, January's hind quarter slid over the cliff. He lunged for her, and the two of them went careening. Through the charcoal darkness and the sand spray around them, he glimpsed the whites of January's eyes glowing with fear.

This dying business isn't so bad, he thought, as they rolled and slid into the pit. He scrunched his shoulders, rounded his chest into a cave and pressed January there. She opened her mouth. An unending scream rose from the back of her throat, spraying spit, covering William in her awful smell.

When the rolling stopped, January jumped off him and ran. Where, William didn't know. He listened until he could no longer hear her paws clawing against the sand. He lay looking up at the stars lining the dome above him, his arms spread like wings. His back hurt like hell, a sure signal he wasn't dead. He imagined his pinkish blood leaking into places it'd never been before. A shiver went through him. So, this was it. This is where he'd take his last breath.

Moving made the pain worse. "I can't be dying," he whispered. "Dr. O'Reilly said that's when the hurting stops." He searched the sky for the brightest star. When he found Bobby Phelps, he said, "Hey. This wasn't supposed to end like this. Guess it's been that kind of week. Nothing's gone right, but I'll make good on it, before the night is over. I'll go out like you did, quiet and brave." With that, he closed his eyes.

William hadn't expected to hear Toady or Dr. O'Reilly up here in the heavens, and for a minute he was confused. Toady's eyes were inches from his face, bugged out as usual. His breath smelled of Tootsie Rolls. "When I found January wandering around by herself, I figured something was wrong. I got Dr. O'Reilly and came as fast as we could."

An ambulance wailed in the distance, and William thought he heard his father and mother. Toady had promised not to tell! His ugly friend stepped aside for the doctor. "Bounma Song Youg O'Reilly, my doctor," William said. She clasped her palms at her heart and bowed. His heart swelled—hands to the heart was a tribute conveying the deepest respect.

"May I touch you?" she asked.

He closed his eyes and smiled. She already had.

MOON TIDE PRAYER

Let us lower the drawbridge for this little one, for he glistens with hope, and inspires each generation to instill in the next values permeated with goodwill. So crucial is this responsibility, if we fail in its propagation, we compromise our hope for the betterment of humanity.

Fletcher William Hart's journal entry: July 12, 1930,
written upon returning from Savannah

Torchlight shimmering along the veranda of the Grand Mitreanna outlined the base of the rambling three-story hotel, from the dance pavilion along its southernmost railing to the crimson-carpeted boardwalk winding around the bathhouse toward the sign for the whites-only beach. That a black man, Fletcher William Hart, stood mere yards from the bold letters crying out against his presence created a sensational attraction. One that bloated the pocketbook of Mr. Fredrick, the hotel's owner, and gave Fletch a paying job when there were few to be had. He pulled a rag from his back pocket and mopped his face from the widow's peak gracing his broad forehead, over the round of his cheeks, down to the troubles anchoring his lips.

From behind the railing on the veranda, the white patronesses of the Mitreanna watched with attentive, yet discreet Southern interest while Fletch staged their evening's entertainment. Naked to the waist and perspired from hoisting shovel after shovel of damp sand into the forms he'd made especially for this show, Fletch's muscular body glistened. "We no better than whores, but what we gonna do?" his wife, Egypt Ann, whimpered earlier this evening as he prepared to leave for work.

Although he dared not look directly at the women, he could feel them staring. From the corner of his eye, he saw them lean into one another, point their gloved hands and whisper. He guessed at the heartless insinuations they were making through their muffled giggles. His wife was right— their imaginations erased the tableau of a poor man earning a night's wages and replaced it with the spectacle of a lion in the throes of mating. Angry heat shot across his chest, down his arms, and into his fingertips. He raised his shovel high and plunged it deeper than ever before. The women inhaled sharply as though...the thought was too terrifying to complete.

Mr. Fredrick smiled at one gentleman and called to another as he strode past the women toward Fletch. Fletch had overheard Mr. Fredrick explain to his new assistant, who'd offered to accompany him down to the beach, that his being alone with the nigger is part of the show. "My guests feel safer when they see me with the beast."

Within a short minute, Mr. Fredrick arrived unsmiling, and unaccompanied by his assistant. Fletch moved his equipment out of Mr. Fredrick's way. "Sandy, my boy, you're late. People threatened to leave if you didn't show."

"Yes sir, I is," Fletch answered, hating his po' boy talk more than the circus nickname Mr. Fredrick had slapped on him.

Mr. Fredrick slid his tuxedo jacket aside and planted his thick palm on his hip. "Hotel's full up and tide's coming in fast." As he spoke, his round belly pushed against the black pearl buttons on his pleated white shirt. He returned his gaze to the veranda, where, bathed within auras of golden torchlight, small groups were seated on velvet chairs around linen-draped tables.

Fletch swallowed. Mr. Fredrick was checking the crowd for indications of boredom—the start of a quick game of cards, excessive drinking, women signaling their husbands for the keys to their rooms—any of which could sound the death knell for Fletch's act.

Mr. Fredrick brightened, waved to a gentleman at the far end of the veranda, then looked up at Fletch, and scowled "You've never been late before. What's happening to you, Sandy?"

Fletch respectfully averted his eyes. "I be tryin' my best, sir."

"Make sure tonight's show is better than your best." Mr. Fredrick brushed the sand from his cuffs, and marched toward the boardwalk, shouting greetings as he went.

He climbed the staircase to the palm-lined entrance of his hotel. In the center, a glass bowl rested on a table, the top of which rode the backs of two regal lions. He faced the crowd gathered along the railing. "Ladies and gentlemen, tonight we have a first at the Grand Mitreanna—the highest tides in history will wash the shores of the Mitreanna as Sandy the Sandman attempts to build a three-story castle at the edge of the sea. Yes, folks, tonight you will witness the Sandman compete with Mother Nature." Necks craned toward Fletch. Mr. Fredrick stretched his arms wide and the whispering settled. "There's more. My bet says tonight's tide will destroy the Sandman's castle *before* he finishes it."

Nervous laughter rippled through the guests. Mr. Fredrick grasped a five-dollar bill by its edges, raised it above his wispy hair, and turned slowly to his left, then to his right. When the oohs and ahhs subsided, a tuxedoed waiter took the bill, set it in the bowl, and lifted a silver tray. He held the tray while Mr. Fredrick chose one pen from several, unscrewed the cap, and wrote his name in the register and beside it, his wager. The crowd applauded.

"Ladies and gentleman, the betting has officially opened: Sandy the Sandman versus the moon tide." The waiter offered the tray to the first gentleman to step forward.

Other nights, Mr. Fredrick's familiar attempts to heighten the evening's tension didn't worry Fletch. Tonight, however, as he'd unhitched his old mule from her wagon and hid her in the barn far from the shiny coupes parked like crooked teeth along the avenue, he heard the thrum of dissatisfaction. From the far edge of the veranda, a little boy cried out, "He's here, the Sandman's here." Ordinarily, Fletch allowed himself plenty of time in which to build a solid base for his castle. But this evening he'd had difficulty pulling himself from his daughter's bedside and feared, with the way Belle was slipping in and out of consciousness, by the time he bought her the medicine she needed, heaven would claim her sweet smile.

Strong and quick, he could make up for being late as long as he ignored the distractions vying for his attention. He hurried, tamping sand into the base form, sprinkling salt-water over the dry spots, and filling the remaining gaps with moist sand. He tightened his grip on the long handle of the tamping tool and leaned hard, sending the force of his two hundred pounds downward onto the flat wooden square he'd attached for just this purpose.

He pressed with all his might and muttered, "Egypt Ann was right. What made me think Dr. Rovner would come to see a black man's child?" Instead, he'd sent a signed Original Prescription Form for Medicine, F281776, and the address of a pharmacist twenty miles away who would fill it for Fletch, if he arrived while Savannah slept. The city was five hours one way, depending on the liveliness of his old mule. He reminded himself that first he had to earn the money to pay for the medicine Belle needed. He finished squeezing air pockets from the base of his castle, and headed past the dunes by the boardwalk to get the forms for the second tier.

Two years earlier, he and his brother, Hugh, calculated the dimensions for this castle. They built the forms and tested them on the far side of the Martons Island fishing pier, beyond the skeleton of a grounded ship, on the Negroes-only section of the beach. That afternoon, after they'd finished building their three-story castle, Hugh dug a moat down to the water. Gentle waves washed hermit crabs, coquina, sponge, and feathery seaweed into the moat. Fletch arranged shells into a coat-of-arms and pressed it into the wall of one of the turrets. He planted a small American flag on one side of the driftwood drawbridge and Georgia's flag on the other. They laughed. The seven-foot structure drew the attention of the guests on the Grand Mitreanna side of the pier. Soon, Fletch and Hugh were surrounded by a sea of curious white faces.

Mr. Fredrick bustled through the crowd. "What's going on here?" he demanded, rolling and loosening his shoulders in readiness to defend his patrons from this Negro annoyance. When he saw the castle and took note of his guests' enchanted expressions, he changed his approach. "Ladies and gentlemen..." he edged closer to Fletch, whose dark skin was sprinkled with sand "...I'm delighted to announce that I have arranged to hire the Sandman to build his extraordinary fortresses on our side of the beach." The crowd broke into hearty applause. "A dollar says the tide takes the castle away by six o'clock," one ruddy-faced gentleman in a damp bathing costume shouted. "My dollar says six-fifteen," said another. Sandy the Sandman had been born.

Fletch jumped on the lowest rung of his ladder, stepped down and pounded sand around its wooden legs until they stood firm. How he wished someone would do the same for him. Perhaps he'd rediscover the confidence he'd basked in after Dr. Rovner had openly admired the carpentry Fletch had completed in the library of the doctor's new home. Convinced of the good doctor's sincerity, Fletch was certain Dr. Rovner would find a way to see Belle, despite the Jim Crow laws. "Not what white folks are inclined to do." His wife's words chided as he reached for the wooden form for the next tier of his castle. Now the work became dangerous. Once he found his footing on the slick ladder, he would lift a brimming bucket of sand over the edge of the form and empty it, without disturbing the lower tier, falling, and making a fool of himself. Again.

The taller the castle, the more difficult to build. He and his brother had made several attempts at ungainly castles, all of which collapsed under the weight of the third tier. Finally, Hugh increased the castle's base to a four-by-four square that was a hefty three feet deep. He narrowed the second tier to a three-by-three, and added a taller deuce as the third, and least stable, tier. With torches burning on either side of the moat and flags flying, the finished castle had been impressive, indeed.

The misty air temporarily distorted Fletch's vision. At first, he thought he recognized the black man running toward him, a jug clutched in one hand and small sack in the other. Whoever he was, the newcomer handed these items off to Fletch, huffed, "Sandwiches from Mr. Fredrick," and sprinted into the shadows. Ladies in evening dresses and shawls twittered at this Negro marathon.

Anxiety, the human version of thunderclaps before a storm, rippled through the crowd. What did they expect him to do, tear into the sack with his teeth? The last he'd eaten was breakfast, and, had this been a different crowd and another less crucial situation, he'd have reached into that sack and devoured this meal. Instead, he placed it to the side. Mr. Fredrick had never sent him food before, and this made Fletch more wary than ever. He'd learned a lesson from Dr. Rovner; never again would he put a black man's hunger on display.

Just then, two young boys came toward him, kicking and chasing a ball. The ball was skittering across the sand when a gust of wind catapulted it toward his half-built castle. The boys froze.

Fletch clutched the bucket of cold, wet sand to his chest and continued to climb the ladder, where, from the next-to-top rung, he could watch the children without being obvious. God forbid anyone were to catch him looking at white children; the boys' hysterical mothers would rile the crowd and create a deadly situation for a nigger. In no time, Jim Crow enforcers, men who'd stored their white robes in the backs of their coupes and on the floorboards of their Model T trucks, would gladly employ him for a different kind of amusement. After all, what would be more entertaining than a moon tide lynching?

The wind teased the blond boy's curls, tossed them this way and that, while the other boy's straight dark hair stood on end. The dark-haired boy spoke a few words to his companion, then nudged him in the ribs. At which, the fair-haired child yanked off his jacket and, with the flair of a circus clown who'd just entered center ring, spun it in the air and released it. He glanced at his friend, took three dramatic breaths and burst into a run. Sand sprayed from the soles of his small churning feet. Waves exploded on the sand bar.

Fletch checked the high-watermark on the breakwater. The tide was coming in fast. If he worked steadily, he'd finish before the waves flushed his moat and eroded the base of his castle. Like it or not, today he was more caught up in the betting than usual: if he finished ahead of the tide, his take of the purse increased from five to ten percent. If not, his efforts went the other way—out to sea, along with the chances of little Belle recovering, and her mother forgiving him for forgetting who he was.

The little boy ran head down into the wind toward Fletch. His friend had, no doubt, dared him to retrieve his ball before the Sandman captured and buried him, and it, within his castle.

Sand swooshed from Fletch's upturned bucket into the second tier. If he hurried, he could tamp it, fill in the uneven spots, and set up the third tier. With luck, he would soon plant the flag of the proud state of Georgia in the top turret, and the crowd would cheer. Not for him, but for Georgia and themselves. He, Fletcher William Hart, was a mere fly that happened to hatch in their midst. He needed to keep that in mind. He banned all thoughts of his brilliance, of reading and writing at the age of three, and later secretly studying philosophy, history, literature and mathematics. He touched his back pocket in which he kept the acceptance letter he'd received from Harvard University. There, he'd assured Egypt Ann, the color of a man's skin didn't matter. But she wasn't interested. All she wanted was for him to fill the prescription he'd tucked inside his ticket to a better life.

Fletch scrambled down the ladder and grabbed the tamping tool. The crowd gasped. Ladies covered their mouths, their eyes widened with horror. A distraught woman — most likely the blond boy's mother—pounded her husband's arm and sent him sprinting toward the boardwalk leading down to the beach. A woman in a flowery dress put her arm around the boy's mother. Little actions had taken on enormous meanings.

Sensing that he appeared to be armed, Fletch set his tamping tool aside. Another ripple rose from the crowd. He rubbed his back, picked up his dinner sack, and sauntered toward the breakwater. The crowd released an audible sigh of relief. His ploy worked.

He made a show of plunging his hand into the sack, knowing its rustling could never be heard above the waves crashing and men shouting, urging the boy to give up his trajectory. "Take off your shoes, so you can run," a woman screamed. Even with Fletch chomping on his sandwich, the father closing in on his son, the boy heading toward his father's rescuing arms, the boy's mother grew more hysterical.

The boy, who had by now sensed his mother's concern and became concerned himself, slipped and fell, then scurried to his feet, and raced even faster toward his father, far from whatever was terrifying his mother. The father lifted the boy and swung him around while the boy laughed with relief. "Papa, put me down," he said and, wiggling from his father's grip, retrieved his ball, and sped toward his sobbing mother. The mother clutched her son to her breast. The crowd's cheering funneled into a raucous obscene roar. By then, the other boy had, at the frantic pleading of his parents, abandoned his friend and returned to the safety of the boardwalk.

So this is how it starts, Fletch thought, angry at the whites for sowing seeds of contamination in yet another generation, angrier with himself for being party to it. That the crowd showed no interest in examining the senselessness of the drama they'd witnessed left him exhausted. Appalled.

He stuffed the remainder of his sandwich into the sack and hurried back to his castle. There was no way, no way in hell, these people would derail the completion of his castle.

But first, Fletch grabbed six empty canning jars with MASON in raised glass letters on each and ran to the boardwalk. The women drew back from the railing. He lined his jars in a row and pressed a sign into the sand behind them.

On his way back to his castle, the light-haired boy, who'd been used to fuel their bigotry, read the sign aloud: "Tips gratefully accepted. Thank-you kindly." Perfectly read. Sadly satisfying.

Fletch worked quickly to finish the second tier. Then he lifted the wooden forms for the third and held them in his outstretched arms. The muscles in his shoulders quivered. Tonight they ached more than usual. He moved his head from side to side, trying to release the tightening that made his temples throb. Miraculously, he lowered the forms into the exact position. He filled bucket after bucket of sand and carried each, without slipping, up the ladder. After completing this last tier, he unlatched the hinges and, slowly, cautiously, so as to keep the work he'd done intact, removed the forms.

They were too heavy to toss down from the ladder, although he was certainly tempted. Unwilling to chance the damage this might cause, he balanced the forms on his head and eased his way down. After the show, he would store them under the boardwalk, where he always kept them. For now, he piled them beside his five-foot sandwich board sign. He sighed, grateful Egypt Ann worked as a morning maid at the Mitreanna and not at night. Choking on his humiliation when he was alone was one thing, Egypt Ann seeing him alongside the huge black letters—SANDY THE SANDMAN—was another.

He gouged out a moat and poked his torches into the sand, one on each side of the moat. When he lit them, the crowd crooned. Carried on the moon tide wind, a gentle new force billowed over the railing of the veranda. Fearful of misinterpreting it, Fletch hesitated before accepting this admiration, not that it was intended for a black man, or a man born white, but for accomplishment, that of a fellow human being. His eyes blurred as he fashioned turrets and crowned them with the flags that represented them all. From deep within the crowd, a thunderclap startled them all: "Pay up, the nigger's won."

Fletch's stomach muscles contracted. This bitter victory was another reminder that, despite the letter in his back pocket, he would never be one of the select. The little blond-haired boy's mother joined others clamoring after Mr. Fredrick, who was busily reassuring them, he, too, had lost. The boy stepped away from his mother. Without drawing attention to himself, he turned toward Fletch, slipped his small hand into the air and waved.

WOVEN BUTTERFLIES

Astani and I sit on the floor of her bedroom, legs crossed, elbows on our knees, foreheads within a breath of touching. I ask if she is nervous about marrying Temil, the distant cousin her parents have chosen for her. "Of course not. Only they know what I need." She speaks with authority befitting the first to be engaged. I search her dark eyes for coyness; instead I find the beginnings of distance, the tool Astani will use to ease me away. My heart flails.

"But that is not what you want," I whisper, as though the possibility of Astani's disappointment is more horrifying than my distress. I watch for the turn of her chin, shift of her hips, a blink that signals aloofness, distance's hurtful twin. She gives me no reason to worry my girlish ways will come between us, for now.

My lightheartedness returns and with it, my confidence. I remind her of the wondrous weeks we spent in the far corner of her father's gardens. How, behind a wall of mulberry bushes, we admired the tender swelling of our breasts, mine mere mounds, hers proud little mountains, keepers of the first womanly longings of her heart.

I'd made up a song about Astani entrusting me with her secret. She closes her eyes and listens as I hum. I've not told her what I'm humming about, nor will I. I can't chance her thinking I'm too childish to understand her desire to leave Afghanistan and travel to Denmark, walk its cobblestone streets, eat fish from its North Sea—all with Amir by her side.

"Yes, think of it. Had we been born in Denmark, we'd be free to choose our own husbands." Astani's tantalizing voice belies her rebelliousness. "Amir for me. Temil, perhaps for you?" She raises her eyebrows and peers into my now fretful soul.

This freedom she speaks of frightens and attracts me at the same time. "I've no desire for Temil," I assure her, rearranging my legs and moving away from her in one deft fold. I hope she hasn't noticed I'm no longer beside her, but she has.

She pulls a tiny scimitar-shaped knife from her pocket and raises it like a slipper moon. The teasing glint in her eyes has dulled. There is a gravity to her, a change I'm not prepared for. "I've wished for something that's against the Qur'an. I've met Temil and his family. I've thanked my parents for making a good match for me. I can no longer dream of Amir. We must vow not to speak of him again." Without hesitation, she slides the blade across the pad of her left thumb. We wait a moment. In that time, I pray she has failed to cut herself. Just as I am about to proclaim there can be no oath without the exchange of blood, a red line appears, dark and undeniable. Astani is on one side; I am on the other.

Careful not to disturb the quivering droplets, she reaches with her uncut hand for mine, places it palm side up on her knee, then slices. I wince and pretend I'm undisturbed by a cut that is deeper than hers.

Astani presses her thumb to mine. I wince again. "Swear to me," she says in a threatening voice. I'm so astounded by her ruthlessness, I am unable to speak. She presses harder. "Do it."

"I swear never to tell anyone you wished you could marry my cousin." I narrow my eyes while the rebelliousness she wishes to drain herself of mingles with my blood, then lean forward, and push back at her with my words, "Now you swear to me."

"About what?" She struggles to keep the points of her mouth from erupting into a teasing grin, then, looking downward, gives in to it.

She knows which vow I want her to make, and that my patience is as fragile as pounded gold thread. Nonetheless, she fingers the wrinkles on her dress, pretending they must be flattened like the barbs protruding from her simple question. Answering her will snag the trust that binds us; delaying puts too much at risk.

She leaves me no choice, so I answer: "Swear—I'll never tell a soul Fahima showed me a book other than the Qur'an." I stare defiantly at her upper lip, at the shadow that has replaced her once invisible down, its fine dark hairs announcing her body's readiness to bear Temil's children and leave our childish pursuits behind.

A soft sincerity returns to my friend's eyes. Her voice swells with incredulity, "But my oath had to do with foolishness that will soon be forgotten. How can I clear my memory of a place such as Denmark where a woman is able to do as much with her life as a man?"

"Hurry, or our blood will dry."

This time Astani obliges me, and it's my turn to smile. When she finishes repeating my words, she rips her thumb from mine and we bleed. Though it's unnecessary for our second oath to take effect, I milk my cut until a tiny crimson dome appears. Astani jerks my hand away. There is no gush of blood, just a lone drop splattering on the tile floor. Our eyes lock. Mine cloud with arrogance, hers with shock. She surmises a shadow has formed over my heart since I broke my promise to my mother, the owner of the forbidden book. And she is right; sorrow's seed has yet to see the sun. When it does, I will apologize to my mother, who reads to me often.

One day after my mother and I finished reading, I tiptoed to her bedroom doorway as she lifted the tapestry from the wall and removed a rough stone. She cushioned her book in cloth and hid it in the hollow. Later, when she left the house, I took Astani's hand and whispered that the secrets of the universe were in my mother's bedroom. She giggled something about her and Temil. I led her to the tapestry and, with her help, pried the stone from the wall. The wonder on Astani's face was more satisfying than winning a dozen goats; I'd introduced her to a universe beyond the bedroom walls.

This book excited Astani and me, more than her news of her marriage. To my surprise, it made me the victor in our unspoken rivalry. Eager to cast this morsel her way, I'd overlooked the danger. But many faces lurked behind the mask of secret knowledge: some belonged to rebel soldiers who might take our village—what if Astani were to taunt them by remarking about Danish women and their freedom? Then there were the faces of her parents after she refused to reveal the source of that which was forbidden her. What if the soldiers threatened to kill Astani? I remind myself that we have just taken an oath. It will protect us all. But the glow of sweet satisfaction has dimmed; my girlish victory has been tainted with the rancor of others. This is my new knowledge. I bear it alone. It and my punishment are one.

The following day is Astani's engagement party. Before leaving, my father hugs me longer, harder than ever, as if he wants to encase me within his touch. We walk through the bazaar to Astani's parents' home on the other side of our village. My father's full-length white tunic gleams with the sun's brightness. I pretended he is a star, shining high above my head. The dark hairs of his moustache stick out beneath his oval nostrils beyond the arc of his lips. He doesn't smile as readily as he once did. His serious eyes sweep the bazaar searching for someone. Who, I don't know.

I pry a pebble from the sole of my sandal and recall the rumor my father told me about a nearby village whose people, in hopes of buying protection from the rebel soldiers, disclosed the activities of neighboring women. Later, the soldiers forced the villagers to stone these very women. I imagine my mother on her knees, head tucked beneath her bleeding fingers, stones scattered around her. I have put her in danger; I am no better than the dirt on which donkeys relieve themselves. My hand opens in revulsion and the pebble falls to the ground as I scramble for the shelter of the bazaar and the familiar buzz of traders.

A gaily-painted horse-drawn jitney jingles alongside me, then rumbles past. The family jostling from side to side calls my name and promises to see me at Astani's. Grateful for distracting me from my fears, I return their greetings with an enthusiastic wave. They are whisked off by their turbaned driver, who maneuvers them among carts filled with almonds, and mulberries, and shoppers hovering like bees. Vendors, mindful of the dust the jitney has stirred into the air, raise brightly colored fabric above their heads for the women to see. Other than the cloth, there is little green here, only that which is pictured in the book I have betrayed.

Earlier today, when I asked my mother about the Danish women who are allowed to make decisions as if they were men, her eyes glistened. She hesitated as though she wished Amir, who lives in Denmark, a country divided not by knowledge but by water, were here to explain. Revealing photographs of pine trees in my mother's book show feathery green arms supple enough to gather ideas from billowing clouds. Their gentle encouraging motions are like those of my

father, the government worker, who is known among arguing
rival merchant nomads as the prince of fair judgments. Here in
our village in Afghanistan, he is said to be the tree goats
haven't nibbled into a stunted bush. "Perhaps it is all those
green trees that makes Denmark such a desirable country," I
said, taking a last peek before my mother removed her book
from my lap.

She replaced it with a pair of fitted pomegranate-hued
pants, a flowing dress and matching headscarf. "That's why the
Afghan woman wears green on her engagement day. It shows
she intends to bring peace and happiness to her husband-to-be."
Her cheeks moistened as she described the 'tears of separation'
she shed on her wedding day. This was her way of telling her
family how much she was going to miss them. It was another
way of telling me she still did.

I could not imagine being handed out the door of my
parents' home like a bundle of twigs. I ran my fingers along the
nubs in the fabric on the front of my dress. My eyes blurred its
crimson dyes into sunset blazes and pinks, the color of herbed
goat meat. I pressed the dress to my shoulders and hopped and
swayed until it bounced with the rhythm of my dancing. Once I
blinked my tears away, my mother started smiling and clapping
in time with my movements. I could have gone on like this
forever, but she asked to see me in my new clothes. Sure as the
sun rises in the East, she'd stitched this, the most elegant
salwar kameez so I would understand the same womanliness

that had claimed Astani now possessed me. I kissed her and pranced away on that special magic.

The atmosphere in the bazaar feels as though the engagement party has already begun. Women draw chunks of spiced goat meat from skewers and hand them to their clamoring children. Clusters of men drink sweetened tea. The smoke from their cigarettes mingles with that of the grilling meat. Wrinkled grandmothers in ankle-tickling veils scold children about to reach for apples at the bottom of the pyramid on a vendor's cart. These scenes are not found in the villages in Denmark, where such activities take place inside buildings behind closed doors. I try to imagine a Danish engagement party without the buffer of these sights and smells. I can't.

My mother's *jilbab* coat swishes past the stall where she bought the velvet *hijab* draped over her dark hair. When she stops to admire an aluminum water container being hammered into shape, or a much-longed-for brass spoon, I trace the swirls on her scarf. Its shimmering white fabric is so fine it wouldn't surprise me if she were to honor Astani by giving her this to wear on her wedding day.

I tap my mother's arm, warmed from the sun. "If our cousin Amir takes a wife, will we travel to his engagement party?" She replaces the spoon quickly, as though it was overheated from the sun. But the spoon's heat isn't what surprised her. I'm afraid she's discovered I've betrayed her confidence.

The suspense is too much to tolerate. "What is it?" I ask. Without answering, she looks at my father, walking slowly from vendor to vendor, hands clasped behind his back. He examines each stranger before turning his gaze to my mother and me. When he comes to an alleyway, he slows his steps, peers in, then continues. He calls for us to wait before we turn the corner to Astani's home. Sounds of the throng mulling there echo down the row of chalky houses, and envelope us within a deafening din. My father joins us for a moment, then hurries ahead. By the time we catch up, Astani's mother and father are moving from guest to guest, greeting, and thanking each for coming to their celebration. They've invited so many people it's a wonder anyone is left to shop in the bazaar.

As my parents exchange pleasantries with another government worker, my mother's face softens with cordiality. She has put my transgression aside but will speak of it later, I am certain. When she does, I hope to be strong enough to accept her anger as the just product of my wrongdoing. Then it occurs to me: we won't find a quiet moment until after the party ends. My guilt has been muffled. I skip off to find Astani.

Her sisters and aunts, who will remain by her side until she and Temil are engaged, surround her. More than ever, Astani looks like a woman. Her dress, the iridescent green of the dragonfly's wings in my mother's book, cascades off her shoulders and over the round of her hips. The whites of her eyes sparkle. Her eyebrows disappear beneath the gold medallion her jeweler father created to honor this occasion.

Each side of this pearl-studded disk dangles from strings of tiny golden beads that connect it to her shimmering green *hijab*. Astani usually greets me with hugs and chatter. Today, her arms are pinned to her sides, her pink lips wrenched into a silent half smile.

Though I can no longer speak of it, I think about Astani and Amir. I once asked her why she would want the short, thick-chested Amir rather than the tall, graceful Temil. "Because he would take me to another place," she said. I reminded her with her new family's wealth, she and Temil would have no difficulty journeying to distant lands. She scowled. Perhaps she did love Amir after all. With this western notion swirling about in my head, I turn my gaze to Temil.

In his dark suit and tie, he looks very handsome, indeed. His shoulders are broad and thin. His jacket tapers at his hips, ending midway along his slender thighs. Temil's intelligent eyes glow with the shy steadiness that says he is ready to take a wife. In the weeks and months before their wedding, he will learn about Astani, perhaps even grow to love her.

A ripple of jealousy runs through me. I tell myself the love of a man for a woman must be more powerful than that of two girl cousins. Yet I fear for Astani. What if Temil doesn't grow to love her as I have? What will become of her playfulness, her beautiful heart?

There is a commotion among the guests whose bright clothing hides the espaliers clinging to the cumin-colored walls in the courtyard. The crowd separates for Temil, his father and mother, who join Astani and her parents. Gesturing hands wilt. Noisy conversations fade one by one like goat herders' campfires on the hillsides before dawn. My skin tingles with envy. From his pocket, Temil produces a gold engagement ring. He places it on the middle finger of Astani's left hand. This is the first he has touched his skin to hers. Temil holds her hand palm down. This way he sees only the upper part of her slender fingers; the scar on her thumb is hidden.

Yesterday, my mother asked about my cut. I couldn't lie, I told her Astani and I had sworn an oath. "An oath is such a serious thing. What secrets could you two possibly have that require an oath?"

I tried to sound carefree as though it was nothing more than a girlhood prank. "If I were to tell you, then I'd violate our oath," I said, praying she wouldn't press me further. I lowered my gaze to the woven butterflies along the hem of my mother's skirt and hoped she'd not read the betrayal in my eyes.

"I see," she said with much respect. This made me feel even more disloyal. She readied the *nan* she'd made to bake in the village ovens. Even though Astani had vowed to never speak of it, I wished I'd not shown her the small cave in my mother's bedroom wall. Women had been stoned for less.

My mother brushed the flour from her hands and touched her fingertips, first to her forehead, then to her heart. I worried she was telling me she understood my misdeed. Perhaps in my haste, I hadn't replaced her book exactly as she kept it. Perhaps I'd left the stone askew, or the tapestry. Perhaps I wanted to give myself away. Her eyes wandered to her bedroom and back to me. She seemed distracted as though something very dear had been disturbed. As much as I wanted to throw my arms around her, I dared not move any closer.

Astani's ringed hand catches my eye. She slips it beneath her *hijab* and above her heart, toward the pin that holds the ring her father made. He'd woven strands of fine gold into an intricate design to show his satisfaction with this match. "Through it, our families will prosper," he said.

She unfastens the pin and hands it to her mother, who closes it within her palm. Astani takes Temil's hand, touching her skin to his. Other than this, they may not touch one another until they are man and wife. The thought thrills me like no other. I wish I were standing in Astani's place. With that, I believe I understand what my mother's sorrowing eyes have been saying. She has started to grieve for she knows I will soon be ready to take a husband. Then I will no longer be hers.

The sun intensifies the heat from the bodies around me. Delicate perfumes fill my nostrils until pungent odors overwhelm them. *Nan,* fragrant with caraway seeds, combines its lovely smells with those of lamb in turmeric, nutmeg and cardamom sauce. *Bouranee baujaun,* Astani's favorite eggplant preparation and *chakah,* a yogurt dish, are also being laid out in readiness for the celebration to come.

Astani takes one scant step away from her father and positions herself in front of Temil. At the same time, her mother slides to the side between them, against her heart, the

Qur'an from which Astani will read. This Qur'an, the only book Astani is allowed to handle, is a special gift from her father. Hand-painted by one of the local artists, colorful images of vines and birds flutter up and down the sides of its pages. She adjusts the angle at which her mother is holding the holy book and smiles shyly. A scowl tugs at her mother's brow then disappears. She is not alone in her concern; I, too, notice Astani's eyes. During her practice recitations with me, she was flawless. Now that she is going to commit herself, her eyes are twitching. I lean forward, willing her nervousness to take flight. My thoughts assure her, *This reading will be like you, a reflection of beauty and pureness.* My uncensored words reveal the problem I have been trying to ignore; in showing Astani my mother's book, I have robbed my friend of the purity today's ceremony is intended to honor. Beads of perspiration form on my forehead and Astani's.

The guests have become aware of the delay and their gaiety has changed to concern. They crane their necks for a glimpse of Astani's refusal to meet Temil's troubled eyes. She looks pleadingly at me, and I shrug helplessly. How can I explain that once you toss aside the monocle through which you viewed your world, there is no antidote to Denmark's twitching distractions? The thin pages of the Qur'an slip from between her fingertips. Her father relieves her mother of the unread passages angled between her daughter's glance and mine and kisses the holiest of books once, twice, three times. A gasp issues from some of the guests. Others shift restlessly. But

Astani is not paying attention. She turns from her father toward the gate through which all his guests have passed. The distant look in her eyes tells me what has happened; my mother's book has forced her to make a passage of her own.

The earth trembles, then spews bowels of dust and debris. Food rains from the sky. The cumin-colored walls disintegrate. The entrance to the courtyard is no more. Bodies that were pressed against me scatter, some screaming, others crying, gagging, coughing. Astani's father whisks his daughter and wife behind him, and pushes his guests aside with his delicate jeweler's arms. I look for my father; I want him to do the same.

"A bomb," a man yells.

Separated from her father, Astani makes her way toward me. For one glorious moment, I am elated; she is coming to get me just as she did in the days when she cared only for me. Her eyes are steady and bright against the powdery film that covers her face except where her medallion, dangling down her cheek, has scraped her skin clean. She rips her medallion off and, without looking at me, presses it into my hand, and rushes into the chaos.

Temil is behind her. "Get water, bandages, a doctor," he shouts to no one in particular. Astani waits for Temil, and they go off together.

Once again, I am humiliated by my childish desire to return to the life Astani has outgrown. It is gone, and so are my mother and father, who are nowhere to be seen. Surely, they must be searching for me, and this comforts me against

Astani's dismissal. How I wish I hadn't separated myself from them. I fear for their safety. Wails of mourning have already begun. I cover my mouth with a portion of my headscarf, and, elbowing my way through neighbors and acquaintances, ask, "Have you seen my mother and father? My father, the government worker, do you know where he is? Did you see a woman in a white *hijab*?"

Their mouths hang open like the dead. My patience is that of a gnat; I want to shake the answers from them, but their shocked faces pose questions of their own. I pray to Allah that my mother and father haven't shared the fate of those being named in the now ceaseless keening. Fearful tears stream down my cheeks. If anything were to happen to my mother and father...the thought tears at my heart, trembling like a small child lost within a woman's breast.

Human blood, once hidden from view, is spattered over the courtyard walls. People from the bazaar who, a short while ago, offered me a tasty apricot or a brass bell, now shove me aside. I brace my feet against their onslaught, absorb the thoughtless blows bruising my feelings. Whoever exploded this bomb has, in one instant, caused many changes. Already I see them. My fellow villagers and I no longer share kindnesses; we panic, each clawing for themselves and their own.

I see my mother and cry out. When she doesn't hear me, I call after her, but she wanders deeper and deeper into the crowd until I lose sight of her. In front of me, two old women cling to one another, take a step, and stop. I grab their arms, sink my fingers into their soft flesh. "Move aside," I say with a snarl. They stare; unspeakable anguish lodges itself within the lines on their faces. My conscience whispers, "Don't hurt them," yet I shove them from my path. We've become animals. I am the worst of the pack.

There is nothing left to the walled entry to Astani's home but a debris-littered hole. The sun in its meanness intensifies the stench; bile rushes up my throat. I swallow a mouthful of bitterness, pinch my nostrils, and breathe through my mouth. All around people are doubled over, vomiting. Astani is also bent in two, her legs spread wide. She claws furiously at the disrupted earth. Temil lowers himself into the hole, and helps Astani uncover the limp legless body of a young girl. He lifts the child's torso to her father's waiting arms. As the father clutches his daughter to his chest, his face contorts with grief. The horrified mother reaches for the little body. As he hands her off, he is startled by how little she weighs. All he has left is smeared on his tunic. His dazed look catches my disrespectful stare. I have intruded on this, his most private of moments. Embarrassed, I hurry off, awash in the twisted confidence that had that been me, my father would cherish my mark on his tunic.

As though I'm waking in the best dream this nightmare has to offer, I hear my father's voice shouting my name, coming closer and closer. When I turn, he presses me to him. Dust from his tunic mixes with my salty tears. His heart pulses with relief. I cling to him, wanting to laugh, scream, and weep all at once.

Within seconds, my mother crushes her body against mine. I reach under her *hijab* for a handful of her hair, and with the other, grab a fistful of my father's tunic. We are an island surrounded by the scrambling of families less fortunate than ours. Together, my mother and father and I are safe. This is where I belong.

As others pass, they jostle my father, who is on his knees, fingers pattering the crown of my head, my eyes, mouth, shoulders, arms, hips, legs, down to my sandaled feet. He rights himself saying, "Thank Allah, there's not a scratch on you." But he's not as pleased as I expected. His burdened expression warns that a decision is about to befall me. He grasps my shoulders, and passes me to my mother. "Take her home and get her ready."

My mother nods. "You have what you need?" she asks, her voice thin and obedient, so unlike the one she uses when reading her book aloud.

He shields his pocket with his right hand. "Yes. I'm to pay half today and half when Amir sends us word of her arrival." Face to face, they recite the vows they whispered many times before. At last I understand the breathy words I strained to hear at night when my father assumed I was asleep: "leave...travel...pay for passage." Now I must face what my heart has been fighting—I am being sent away. Dismissed.

The marketplace is like a child's broken puzzle that has been heaved into the air, and allowed to fall where it will. Holding hands, my mother and I pick our way around the lifeless shanks of vendors' stands. Dust fogs the air, forcing us to cover our mouths, and cough all the way home. When we arrive, my mother takes my hand once more and leads me to her bedroom. The deliberation with which she removes her *hijab* signals the start of a sacred rite. "Do you know what I'm doing, Fahima?"

"I'm not sure," I tell her, my voice fragile as silver bell.

She shakes her headscarf clean. With it against her chest she folds it in half. "This fold is to remind you of your father." She folds it in half again. "This is to remind you of me." She folds it one last time, pressing swirl after swirl over one another. "And this is the three of us together forever in one another's hearts." Her words are strange and beautiful and mysterious. My thoughts swarm, my heart floods, and an indescribable weight wedges itself between the breasts I once so eagerly welcomed.

My mother hands me her *hijab*. Her eyes glisten. "Fahima, this is for you to wear on your wedding day."

I trace the soft smooth patterns hoping they will help me understand why I have leapfrogged from a wedding that was asleep on a star of the future into a ceremony laden with secrets. "Why are we speaking of this now? Who will I marry?"

"Your cousin, Amir, awaits you in Denmark."

"Amir?" His name thickens on my tongue. My mother reads the confusion on my face. The gentle pressure of her hands on my cheeks quiets my trembling. Instinctively, my eyes close, and I concentrate on capturing the memory of her fingertips on my skin. I grieve because my heart tells me I am to be married without my mother and father. Without them greeting our guests. Without them holding the Qur'an, from which I'll read to Amir. Without them seeing my gift of tears, shed to show how much I'll miss them.

My father rushes in, perspiration dripping from his face. "You have told Fahima of our wishes?" My mother nods. He turns to me and flings his hands in the air. "You've seen the work of Taliban rebels announcing their intention to make our village their home. Already they practice their terrors." He whispers as if someone had an ear against our thick walls. "I've arranged for you to travel with friends who have been to Denmark often. They'll bring you to Amir. You'll marry him at once, that way you may live lawfully with him."

Panic rises in my chest. "What about meeting his family? What about an engagement ceremony?" My voice has risen louder than it should. I lower my eyes in apology.

My father takes my head in his hands. "My dear child, customs are meant to help our people flourish, not bind us." His explanation is patient, quiet yet deep. His firmness allows no room for fear.

To seal his words, my mother hands me the Qur'an her mother gave her on her wedding day. "I've marked the passage you're to read to Amir at your wedding." She points to a lock of her dark hair, curling from between its pages. Although my father has excused us from the customary formalities, my mother has need of hers.

All this does little to help me against the sandstorm sweeping me away. "What about you?"

"We'll come as soon as we're able." My father's voice quivers, just a little. An Afghan daughter doesn't question her parents' wishes. I swallow hard, and tell my father I am happy to obey him. He holds me to his chest, and folds my mother into his arms. I let his tunic absorb my tears, and pray to Allah to allow us to do this again. Voices at the door cause us to stiffen. My father kisses me before rushing off.

Ever since the explosion, my hand has been knotted into a fist. I unfold it. There, on my numb palm, beside my scarred thumb, is Astani's engagement medallion. Will my cousin forgive me when she learns I've married Amir? Will she grumble in the depths of her heart that I'm the silent victor, stealing off with the one she loves? I ask my mother if I might return the medallion; I must tell Astani of my new vow—to care for Amir. My mother smiles sadly and says, "There's no time."

She places a pack, weighted with things for the long journey, on my back. Certain Astani and I will hold our friendship forever in our hearts, I slip her medallion into my pocket. My mother takes her Qur'an and *hijab* from me, wraps them in her silky butterfly skirt, and plunges them deep within my pack. I am pulled off-balance. My arms jerk. Outstretched, they are like the wings of the woven butterflies on my mother's skirt, only damp with newness. They hover by my mother, absorbing the drying heat from her body so they will be able to fly.

A TEASPOON OF PERFECTION

Balder's round, honest eyes watched me scooping ash from the bottom of the wood stove in the middle of my kitchen. "Do you want me to do that for you?" he asked.

"Another time, I'm almost done."

He unzipped his fleece vest and settled on the sofa, elbows perched on his thighs, fingertips idle. He was red-faced, gray-haired, wiry, and at this moment, intense. "You make a lousy advertisement, Katie Shields."

"Excuse me?" I asked, snaking my head around.

"You ought to save your wood stove for emergencies." Balder was staring at my hindquarter, probably noticing how much it looked like a horse that was about to kick.

"I'm addicted to the crackle of burning wood. Besides, what are you planning to do? Tell our customers I won't use the same heating oil I pump into their tanks?"

I stood up, and planted my hands on my hips, thought how much simpler life was when I ran the business solo. Before I'd bought my second oil truck, and convinced Philip Balder, my longtime drinking buddy, he could spare some time from his horse farm to drive it. But he surprised me. "Employee isn't good enough," he said. "I want to be your equal partner."

"Commitment's a noble concept," I said, and offered him a forty-nine percent share.

Balder thought for a minute, then we shook hands, and went to The Lobster's Claw to celebrate. He took a napkin from the bar and sketched a picture of Leah, my Irish Wolfhound. Above it, he lettered the name he proposed for our company: 'Balder and the Bitch.'

"Touché," I had said, "But forty-nine percent is the best I can do."

I brushed the ash from my hands. "I suppose you're right about the using the furnace, especially when Mom's visiting."

She must have heard us, because she came out of the guestroom wearing spandex leggings, a T-shirt, and her Nikes. She shivered, took her sweatshirt from the back of the sofa, and slipped it over her L'Oreal blond curls. "I bet Balder would caulk those leaky windows, if only you'd ask," she said.

Balder raised one of his tufted eyebrows into a questioning 'v-shape,' and waited for my reaction.

"I'll take care of it," I said.

They exchanged glances. He leaned over, cupped his hand to her ear, and pretended to tell her a secret. "Skittish, isn't she? The way I figure it, if she won't take my offer to help, then I haven't done a good job of asking." Mom broke into the playful smile she used to share with my father, and nodded.

They giggled while I closed my eyes and shook my head, annoyed, but grateful to Balder for coaxing a smile from her. It had been three months since Mom had phoned with that close-to-hysterical tone in her voice to say Dad had died of a massive coronary; it was good to hear her laugh.

Later that afternoon, I was halfway out of the parking lot at the Downeast Health Club, about to merge with the traffic along Route 1 in Ellsworth, when Mom opened her purse, unzipped one compartment, rifled through it, closed it, and did the same with the next one. "Oh no," she murmured.

"What's the matter, Mom?"

"I can't find my key."

"I have keys to my house."

"No Katie, I've lost the key to your locker," she said, and pulled her lipstick, a comb, her wallet, used tissues from her bag. She unzipped, and searched each compartment again, her seventy-four-year-old fingers moving more frantically with each zip.

"You probably left it in the locker room. We'll go back."

"It's lost, I'll never find it," she said, then lowered her voice to a whisper. "Don't tell your father, please don't tell him what happened."

Mom's words surprised me, like the thunder of lake-ice shifting under my feet. She had occasional memory lapses, but never this severe.

"Mom, look, I'm turning the truck around."

I shifted my gaze from the traffic, and glanced at her. Her eyes were squeezed tight, her lips pursed, and she was pounding the sides of her head with her fists. Horrified, I made a sharp turn into the Mobil station on the corner; behind me, brakes screeched.

"I hate it when my brain forgets things. I hate myself," she said, and continued hitting her head, making her hearing aids whistle.

"Mother, please." I stopped my truck, and took her knobby fists in mine. "It's going to be okay. Don't hurt yourself anymore. Please."

She ran her fingers over the gray braids alongside my oval face, the one in the family photo albums that looked so much like hers had twenty-four years ago. She dropped her hands into her lap and scowled. "It's awful when your father gets mad, he's so…unpredictable."

She was right, Dad had been intense, but what had bothered me more was Mom's acting as though she were his appendage, waiting solely upon his pleasure. Once, at a dinner-dance for the Friends of St. Jude's Home, a photographer from the *Portland Press Herald* was gathering the big wigs to take a photo for the society column. My mother and I had been deep in conversation with another woman when my father rushed over, exasperated. Without a blink of acknowledgment, he interrupted, "I've been looking all over for you...the photographer's not going to wait forever." He wrapped his arm under my mother's, and jerked her away. She struggled to regain her footing, and scurried after him, her smile intact.

"Don't worry, Dad will never know." I held Mom's fingers tight until she squeezed back, then said, "Let me check your bag."

She watched while I rummaged through her things, then pulled out my key. "You found it," she said, her face bright with relief.

I glanced at the dashboard. On it was a copy of *Active Retirement,* with its cover photo of a silver-haired couple, each straddling a mountain bike; beneath, in bold print, "Testing for Dementia: What to Expect." Balder had given it to me this past summer, after my father had scheduled an appointment for Mom at the Geriatric Clinic in Portland. He'd told her the doctor had ordered some testing. She worshiped her woman doctor, and would have trained to climb Everest if Dr. Budjanii had prescribed it. I hated the way my father had tricked her, and that he hadn't noticed she was having trouble until she couldn't remember how to make lasagna—his favorite dish.

"Anything new with Balder?" Mom asked, breaking the silence on the way home. I'd made the mistake of telling her that Balder had hired a manager for the farm, so he could spend more time at our office, and that he wanted to marry me.

I tried to sound casual. "Not a thing. Balder's still my business partner, nothing more."

A half-hour later, we bounced down the dirt road towards the Blueberry Fortress. That's what Mom had named my two-story home, built like a moatless castle by an eccentric architect in the middle of a blueberry patch overlooking Cadillac Mountain. The first floor is as open as a bowling alley, with a spiral staircase leading up a tower to the most beautiful spot in the house, my master bedroom. Leah and I sleep there beside the sliding glass doors. Each morning, after I open my eyes to the bristly-faced mountain, we step onto the deck, and watch the finches and chickadees darting from the nearby spruces to my feeders, and back.

Mom put her hands on the dashboard, leaned forward, and said, "It's perfect." She used the same words the first time she'd seen my house. They had stunned me, since I expected her to be disappointed that I hadn't used the money from my divorce settlement to buy something more conventional, like the colonial she and my father lived in.

She sat back. "But there is something missing," she said, twisting her wedding band.

I braced myself. "What's that, Mom?"

"A man." She got that starry look in her eyes, the one that always came before a mother-daughter moment, then said, "You can have all sorts of material things, Katie...a truck, a business, a house, but they can never replace a man."

Static whistled from the radio. Grateful for the distraction, I fiddled with the dial, then pointed to Leah, waiting by the mailbox at the end of the driveway. She ran along side us, keeping pace with the truck's twenty-five miles per hour, her ivory head level with my window, her tongue spewing spit. "She's galloping, like a miniature horse," Mom said.

She seemed delightfully childish, and I wondered about this becoming a problem. Her doctor had reassured my father that she didn't have Alzheimer's. "Short-term memory deficit" was the term he'd used. It made me want to weep, knowing all I could do was hang on tight as Mom yo-yoed between confusion, and knowing exactly what she was doing.

"I wonder if Balder misses his farm," Mom said.

I recalled this morning's banter between Balder and my mother, and my hands tightened around the steering wheel. I wondered if he'd lose interest if I didn't maintain the independent filly routine. Wondered what he'd do if he knew it didn't come naturally, and that I had to work damn hard to avoid being like my mother.

I parked the truck by the granite ledge on the side of the house. Leah pressed her spotted nose against the window, and her breath froze on the glass as we listened to predictions of our first snow. "A nor'easter," the announcer's voice said. I turned off the engine, and Mom dangled my locker key in front of her, then dropped it my hand.

I wrinkled my nose, and nodded as if to say, "Getting old sucks, and there's not a thing we can do about it." This was Mom's first visit without my father. She seemed wobbly, like a kid trying to balance her two-wheeler without its training wheels. A kid who needed me to keep one hand on the handlebar, the other on the seat, and run beside her, ready to catch her, if she were to fall.

When I let Leah into the house, she headed up the spiral staircase and howled for me to open the doors to the deck. "Go ahead, guard the fortress," I said, and she stepped outside. The air had that damp, cold smell that comes before it snows, and my nose told me we're about to have a storm of blackout proportions.

I left Leah outside, and sank into my waterbed. It had been the first thing I bought when I left my husband. After eighteen years on the same mattress, I'd asked him to buy a new one, like the ones I'd seen on TV. He refused, called me "a soft sell," the type every advertising agent dreamed of. The water in the individual tubes made a lonely sloshing sound as I rolled toward my bedside stand, picked up the phone, and dialed the office.

Balder answered, "Blueberry Oil Distributors." Lyle Lovett, his favorite CD, played in the background. Mom and I had once argued about how hard it would be for a woman my age to get used to living with someone else. She assured me it'd be easy to let Balder's tastes and habits become my own. "First, he'll try to teach you the Texas two-step, and you'll wonder if you'll ever stop tripping over his feet. Then one day, you'll find yourself gliding along, humming his favorite tune."

I pictured his lanky six-foot-two in his survival suit, unzipped to the waist, steel toe boots on the desk, a cigarette burning in the soup bowl he used for an ashtray, phone cradle resting on his collar bone. I wanted to tell him about the key incident. About how Mom asked me not to tell my dead father, but I hesitated, afraid if I said the words out loud, it'd confirm what I already knew, and I'd wind up like Mom, pretending it didn't matter.

Balder named the new customers who'd signed up for oil delivery, and went on to tell me how Fibber, the dog down the street from the office, had been hit by a car. "He's okay. I brought him to Dr. Carly's," he said, and started describing what had happened.

There was a loud, hollow sound on the other end of the line; Balder's feet had dropped to the floor. I could hear him moving around the office. The music changed to my CD, Tommy Makem's, *The Lark in the Morning*. It was one of the songs the band had played during my father's retirement party at the Portland Country Club, three weeks before his heart attack. Two hundred people applauded when I introduced my gift: Jamie McCallum, Pipe Major, in full dress regalia. His green and blue plaid kilt swished to the beat of *Minstrel Boy*, while he marched back and forth in front of my father. Dad stood at attention, and as his favorite, *Bonnie Lass*, droned, he stared at me.

From where I stood on the other side of the room, I could see tears glistening on Dad's face, and I had wanted to go to him. Wanted to tell him that thirty years and one wrecked marriage had given me plenty of opportunity to compare my ex-husband's need for other women with my father's need for my mother. And that, by comparison, he'd come out on the positive side of my equation. But the piper played a strathspey, and someone called for Dad and Mom to lead the dancing, and my chance got lost in the next reel.

I thought about last night, and how I chanced losing again. Balder had wanted to talk about us, but I said, "It's only been four years since the divorce; my life is just beginning to feel right." I knew Balder was "right" but didn't know if he'd be perfect. Didn't know if I could tolerate not having perfection this time, didn't want to risk exploring it.

Balder stopped talking, and I chatted about today's session at the health club, and what great shape Mom was in. "By the way, I wondered what you thought of having a party tomorrow night for my mother? It'll be her seventy-fifth birthday. I'm going to make lasagna and a cake."

"Sounds good, Katie, but do you think she's in the mood for a party? It's only been three months since she buried your father." Balder sounded cautious, weighted by his inclination to avoid taking sides in the battle over old hurts. His somber expression reminded me of the day I'd told him about my ex-husband, and how he'd gone out, left me home in bed, hemorrhaging after my hysterectomy.

Balder told me I'd never have to worry, he wasn't that kind of man. "Prove it," I'd said, as we hiked up the carriage trails in Acadia National Park. Balder had left college to take a job, he told me, his green eyes sad and still. I knew he'd never married, and I asked him why. He called her a gold-digger, a co-ed who'd lied about taking the pill. I imagined Balder at the end of his weekly visits with his little boy, watching him walk towards his mother's door. Then later, at his desk in his farmhouse, writing a check, one each month, until his son had finished his degree.

I got angry. At that sponging bitch; at my father's leaving me so unexpectedly; at Balder's telling me what to do; and most of all, at myself, for being so goddamned terrified that what's happened to my mother is what's going to happen to me.

I snapped into the phone, "We're not going to rock 'n roll, stupid. It's going to be a quiet dinner party." As soon as the words came out, I wished I could snatch them back. But it was too late, and besides, I could use some distance between Balder and me. But the gap felt bigger than I'd expected.

On the other end of the phone, Balder blew out smoke, prolonged and emphatic, like the chimney on a factory at quitting time.

"I'm sorry, I shouldn't have said that. It's just that…"

"Don't worry, Katie, I've had kicked sand in my face before. It scratches and makes my eyelids shrivel closed. I'll be the blind man, if that makes you happy. But do me a favor; stop pretending my opinion matters." He sighed. "A party is just what your mother needs. Is that what you want to hear?"

I slammed the phone down because he was right, that was exactly what I wanted to hear. If I'd wanted to pay attention to what he thought, I wouldn't have put him off every time he got close to asking me to marry him. Wouldn't have been so skittish about putting myself in a situation where I might become, once again, the kind of wife my mother had been.

Round and round, my hand glided along the smooth, black railing on the spiral staircase that led to the kitchen. Had I pushed Balder into wanting to swap his hopes of life with me for one with someone smart enough to know that Balder is the name of the Norse god of wisdom and light, someone who'd treat him accordingly?

"Why shouldn't he find someone else?" I asked aloud, amazed at the words' sickening effect. I imagined life without him, and felt as if I'd lost something important, a leg, an eye, my soul, perhaps. I was filled with disbelief, the same horrible wonder that overwhelmed me when I first saw my father from the waist up, lying in the state of perpetual rest.

I needed to do something so I'd stop thinking about Balder. I had a party to get ready for. I opened the pantry, removed several cans of tomatoes, and tried to balance them in the crook of my arm. I moved too quickly, and they rolled off in three directions. The farm girl's picture on the fifteen-ounce can appeared, then disappeared as it careened toward the bud vase and pink carnations Balder had given Mom. The off-level counter made it gain speed, and I stepped to the right, my hand extended, about to scoop it up, when my ankle turned beneath me, and I tumbled to the floor.

"Damn you, Leah," I bellowed. Pain shot from my heel into my ankle, and before clutching it, I hurled Leah's foot-long chew-bone past the wood stove, slamming it into the wall on the other side of the room.

Leah heard the commotion, and threw herself against the sliding glass doors on the deck. My mother's slippered footsteps hurried from her bedroom to my side.

"What happened?" she asked, and inspected my ankle. "It's swelling. I'll make an ice pack." Her voice was clear and in control.

With my hand hooked on the sink, I hauled myself up, my weight on my good foot. I swung the other up on the counter, untied my sneaker, and rested my ankle in a puddle of water. Pink carnations were strewn, as if by flower girls, around my foot.

"It's swelling like a son-of-a-bitch," I muttered from behind clenched teeth.

"What did you say? I need to put new batteries in my hearing aids," my mother said too loudly, then unloaded a tray of ice cubes into a dishtowel, and tied it into a knot. She settled the icepack on my ankle, pulled a chair from the table, and slipped it behind me. Hands on my shoulders, she guided me into the chair.

"Keep your foot there, I'll get a stool." She hurried off to her bedroom, and returned with it, and pillows from her bed. She stacked them, and gently lowered my leg.

"My trainer in Portland said ice and a naproxen tablet will control the inflammation." Mom reached into her pocket for an oval pill tinted robin's egg blue. She ran the faucet, handed me a glass of water, then the pill.

"Thanks, Mom," I whispered. Exhaustion tugged at me, and I gave in to it, unsure if I was more relieved by my mother's presence, or by her being focused enough to take care of me. I placed my elbow on the counter, and rested my head.

The door of the wood stove creaked open. One log thumped against another, then landed on the grate. Embers flared momentarily, like disturbed bees, then settled into their work. Cast iron clinked against cast iron, sealing in the warmth from the heart of the stove, overpowering the cool breezes that had crept, uninvited, into my fortress.

"I'll be back in a minute. I need to get a couple of batteries," Mom said, and ran her hand lightly over the top of my head. Its gentle steadiness sent memories streaming through me of my mother and father leaning over me after I'd fallen from my new two-wheeler. They stroked my chestnut hair, and reassured me that falling down was part of learning, that bruises were the body's way of reminding us to do things differently the next time.

Leah quieted down, and I could hear Mom speaking in the other room. She stopped for a moment, then said, "Yes Balder, that would be very helpful." The rest of her words blurred as I fell asleep.

I awoke to the smells of onion and garlic, simmering in spitting-hot oil. A spoon clinked against the inside of a metal can like a clapper in a tin bell.

I twisted my body toward the stove and grimaced. The ice pack, now in a crinkling plastic bag, fell to the floor, and my ankle throbbed. I propped myself up on one elbow, and squinted at my feet at the other end of the sofa. The footstool was by my head.

"Mom, how'd I get to the sofa?" I asked. My voice sounded little and young, about seven years old, after the doctor had confined me to the house. "A case of glandular fever," he'd said, and told my mother to keep me quiet, and give me plenty to drink. I looked at the footstool to see if Mom had left a glass of ginger ale. Balder's fleece vest was there, instead. I reached out for its sturdy softness.

Mom and Balder poked their heads out from behind the brick hearth. They wore identical aprons; blue canvas with white lettering that read Blueberry Oil Distributors.

"That was quite a tumble you took," Balder said, and knelt by my side.

"It was so stupid," I began, but Balder put his fingers over my lips. He tasted sweet, like basil.

"It was an accident," he said, his tone firm. "But when I found you passed out on the counter, I was really scared."

"Really?"

Mom handed me a glass of ginger ale. "How are you feeling?"

Confused, I wanted to say. I clasped Balder's hand, and let him pull me upright, then took the glass from Mom. Balder lifted the afghan from my feet, and inspected the damage.

"Looks like a bad sprain," he said, his face gnarled with concern. "I've called the emergency room; they're expecting us in half an hour."

The following evening was Mom's seventy-fifth birthday, and I sat on the sofa, with my bandaged foot on the footstool, disappointed that I didn't have a gift. I recalled years ago, when I'd bought her bath towels with enormous sunflowers on them. She tucked them in the back of her linen closet, behind a stack of her solid green towels. Gifts need to fit the person, not the giver, I'd learned; finding the perfect match meant loosening my definition of perfection. I wondered if I'd been able to go shopping, what I would have chosen.

"Can I help, Mrs. Shields?" Balder asked. He leaned against the counter, sipping beer from a frosty mug; an unexpected jealousy ran through me.

"Everything's ready." Mom pulled the lasagna out of the oven, and the aroma of herbs and spices filled the house. I marveled that she had been able to cope with my injury and make the lasagna.

Balder popped ice cubes into a glass. "Who's having a Shirley Temple?" he asked, and shot me a consoling grin. His slender face was a wind-kissed red, and his silver hair ponytailed at the nape of his neck. "Don't worry Katie, you won't need to take codeine for long."

He handed me a glass of ginger ale with an orange slice teetering on its lip, kissed my forehead, and said, "Your Mom and I are going to bring the table in here, so you won't have to move."

I smiled a woozy smile, content to let him care for me. It was a risk associated with taking this painkiller, one little white pill every four hours. "May impair judgment," but I didn't mind. Even with drug-saturated eyes, I could see the happiness on Balder's weathered face. The brownish hue in his green-gray eyes was soft, confident, that of a man who knew he belonged. Who wasn't afraid of the "for worse" part of "for better or for worse." Who wasn't threatened by what might be, who was comfortable with what is.

"It's snowing," Mom said from the kitchen.

"Thanks for being here," I said, and reached for Balder's oil-stained hand; it felt warm and soothing against mine.

Moments later, Balder and Mom inched their way around the hearth, their arms stretched taunt, he squatting to keep the oak table balanced between them. Then Mom slipped into the singed oven mitts by the stove, and lifted the lasagna as if she were carrying the platter for a Boar's Head celebration. Balder stepped aside, raised an imaginary trumpet, and sang, "Dum, da-da, daaa."

They're hamming it up for me, I thought, and swallowed the emotion in my throat. I wasn't used to a man going out of his way for me. Except now that I thought about it, that's all Balder had ever done.

He poured Chianti, my favorite wine, into his and mom's glasses, but not mine. "Do you want some grape juice?" he asked.

I tried to sound stoic. "I'll pass. Someone's got to stay sober." We both laughed out loud, until Mom said, "It was cute, but nothing to get hysterical over," then we laughed even harder. It was my first laugh since my accident, and sharing it with Balder felt good.

"Let's sit down, before dinner gets cold." Mom used the same words she'd said countless times when Dad and I had straggled to the table. Could I hear myself saying those words, here by the wood stove, to Balder? I closed my eyes, strained to listen.

After dinner, the table looked as if locusts had landed. Half the lasagna was gone, and the bread and salad had disappeared. Balder started to clear the dishes. He clasped one stem between his thumb and index finger, and slid the other wineglasses between his fingers. They sparkled like gaudy baubles.

The lights flickered, and the refrigerator motor coughed and sputtered. "Storm must be bringing down the power lines," he said. The northeast winds whipped the nearby pine boughs against the clapboards, and the lights flickered once more, then the house went black, except for the glow from the wood stove.

"What's happening?" Mom asked, panic in her voice.

"Stay in your seat, Mom. Balder's getting the Coleman lantern. It's going to be all right."

A soft radiance filled the room as the god of Light lowered the lantern to the table. Mom's face glowed, and she whispered, "Remember how your father used to tell me to make a wish whenever the power went out? If it came on within the hour, he'd say my wish had been granted." She paused. "It's too bad your father had a trial this week, he would have loved this."

Balder and I exchanged looks. His eyes locked on mine. Now he knew, I thought. I panicked, wanted to get up and go to Mom, but couldn't reach my crutches. My eyes skittered between Balder and Mom.

"Dad's not at a trial."

"I know that, Katie. Sometimes, I like to pretend he's still with us. It's silly, but it makes it easier to tolerate the ache."

"You're right, Mrs. Shields," Balder called from the kitchen. "Sometimes when I'm on the farm, repairing fence posts, I imagine working shoulder to shoulder with my son."

I felt sorry for Mom, but sorrier for Balder. He fathered a son, but never had one; asked for an equal partnership, but got one percent less; offered me love, knowing the most I could give back was a teaspoon of perfection.

"I'm ready to make my wish now," Mom said, and closed her eyes.

I closed mine, too, and thought about giving. I've never been able to find the perfect gift. Maybe that's why we have birthdays every year—to give us another chance to figure out what makes the person we love happy. Eventually, after a few bruises, we let ourselves celebrate whatever fits the person. Sometimes, in the process, we find ourselves loving the gift, too. Mom sighed, and I opened my eyes. I knew what my gift would be.

Balder burst into the room with a cake lit like a torch, and set it in front of Mom. He pretended to look for the key of C on an imaginary pitch pipe, hummed it, and started singing "Happy Birthday."

But Mom looked lost, left out, as if someone told a joke, and she didn't get the punch line. She looked from Balder to me, her smile timid, her penciled eyebrows furrowed in confusion. Leah howled as we sang, "Happy Birthday, dear Mom, Mrs. Shields…" I kept smiling, even though I wanted to cry. For her, comfort came from knowing what to expect. Perhaps that's why she was so certain that a marriage to Balder would work out; in her seventy-five years, she'd developed a sense of what a woman could expect from a man like Balder, and to her, it was okay. I pointed to her and mouthed, "It's for you."

Mom's face brightened, and she blew out the flames from seventy-six candles: seventy-five and one to grow on. "Those roses remind me of the ones that used to come on cakes from Martin's Bakery in Portland. Do you remember, Katie?" Mom asked.

"Um," I said, savoring a fingertip of frosting.

"Remember how you used to peel back the petals on the rosebuds?"

"Remember how I used to wish the bakery would hide tiny gifts in them? And you told me I should send my suggestion to Mrs. Martin?" I slid the rosebud from the cake, and sucked the buttery frosting from its stem, then pushed the first petal back, then the second, and the third.

The lantern flickered like a spotlight on the rosebud. It glittered, and something dropped with a 'cah-chink'. A dime store ring, the kind with the adjustable shank, and a pretend diamond with gaudy, heart-shaped rubies, one on either side, had landed on my plate.

"What's this?" I asked. Mom held her fingertips in prayer position over her mouth and nose. The whistling of her hearing aids was the only answer to my question.

Balder dragged the table back, peeling away my armor, leaving me exposed and vulnerable. He picked up the ring between his thumb and index finger, and fell to his knees on one side of my outstretched leg. His honest, round eyes peered into mine, and he held his ring in his Light.

I knew what he was doing, but was distracted by the corners of his mouth twitching, waiting for my signal to release his smile. I didn't want Balder to wait any more. I reached out and traced his lips.

Balder looked silly, solid, and wonderful, and we laughed when he tried to slip the ring on my finger. He stopped to adjust it so it would slide over my knuckle. I smelled his cake-sweet breath while his fingertips traced the freckles on my cheeks, leftovers from my girlhood, perhaps pretending if he landed on the right one, I'd award him the key to my fortress.

His wiry beard sent loving messages up and down my neck. I combed my fingers through his hair, and started humming. The logs in the stove shifted into new forms, and I glanced at our shadows, dancing a slow dance to the beat of embers settling on the grate.

BROKEN

A mind at war with its heart is one of nature's most destructive forces.

Mother Hart, 1929

Eleven years earlier, hours before Cornelia Hayes gave birth to her first boy, she asked her husband, Thaddeus, to move the chairs from the porch of their small cabin to the grassy patch at the bottom of the steps. Too uncomfortable to sleep through the suffocating Georgian heat, she sat there gazing at the stars. Thaddeus dozed fitfully until she roused him with, "I need the midwife, Mother Hart." After Randolph had been born, Thaddeus returned the chairs to the porch, where they remained until Cornelia was ready to deliver their second child, at which point she asked him to move them, then go directly to Mother Hart's. Mother Hart opened the door for Thaddeus, who blurted, "The chairs are in the grass." The next time Thaddeus babbled about chairs, Mother Hart grabbed her birthing bag, and rushed to help Hayes' baby three and, a year later, baby four join the world. But this mournful July afternoon, as Randolph shouted his news, "The chairs are in the grass," Mother Hart opened her eyes and stared at the ceiling. The

127

more he yelled, the harder it became for her to pry herself out of bed.

* * *

What a sorry time to be born, she thought as Fletch stood by his mule in front of Thaddeus' home, his arm angled where she could reach it, should she feel unsteady. She placed her hand on her son's shoulder and crawled down from the wagon. *When did I start needing him like he once needed me*, she asked herself.

"You think your dizziness is a touch of the fever, Mam?"

"Fever?" she repeated absently. "This is worse."

Fletch scowled with concern. No doubt, her insistence on being here disturbed him. He'd offered to get the white girl, Promise, to come in her place, but Mother Hart declined. Not that the orphan girl wasn't good; Mother Hart taught her all she knew about midwifery, except how to keep the neediness from her eyes when a new baby nursed. Mother Hart was all too familiar with that emptiness; she'd come face to face with it after her husband, William's, hanging. Though she'd mourned, she'd refused to come undone, at least not while her young boys, Fletch, Hugh, and Trivett were watching.

Instead, she tightened her fist around her dignity, forced her face into a tattered smile, and showed them how to live with an aching heart. She didn't want her boys to grow up in the shadow of their father's murder, so she pretended she had put it aside, and helped them to do the same. She'd been the one who'd loved a white man so decent she couldn't bear to let him go; her boys were not to blame for her choice of a husband, although they'd grown up fatherless as a result. That was as far as she'd allow their punishment to go. So she tucked her sorrow inside, without weighing the lessons that grief can teach, without allowing them to practice coming to terms with loss, without imagining that her protectiveness would cripple them when it came to understanding what was happening to her now.

Pride had deprived them, and her, of the cleansing slog through grief's swamp. Worse yet, holding back had fooled them into believing she was so strong, nothing could touch her. For a while, she believed it too, until early this morning, when she'd learned of Trivett's murder. Fletch didn't need to say a word. No sooner had she read the horror in his eyes, than her memories exploded to life, and with them, the urge to unravel. An urge she denied for a second time. The next time Fletch and Hugh were together, consoling one another over yet another loss, she wanted Fletch to marvel to his brother that, despite the battering their mother's heart endured, her mind never faltered. That would be her gift to her adult children, the ones that were still alive, that is. Problem was, with the horrors that had been clawing at her thoughts, she wasn't sure it would be true.

"You sure you're feeling all right? It's not too late to get Promise." Fletch arched his fine eyebrows, and leaned forward, ready to do her bidding.

"The bruises on your brother Trivett's neck are still fresh, and you're going to chance being seen with a white woman?

That's the most foolish thing to ever come out your mouth, Fletcher William." As shame clouded the golden flecks in his brown eyes, she chided herself for lashing him with her pain. *Apologize*, she told herself, but the words jammed the back of her throat, and refused to come forward. *Just one or two, and he'd understand; Fletch is decent like his father*, her thoughts urged. She was about to speak when Fletch put his fingers to his lips, and pointed to the back of the wagon.

There, Randolph Hayes lay curled in an earth-brown ball. Annoyed at having bared her emotions in the boy's presence, she was about to warn him not to repeat her words, when his lips fluttered with soft snores. Thank goodness. She'd convinced Fletch this wasn't the time to tell his parents, Thaddeus and Cornelia; with the baby coming, the next few hours would be trying enough. They would tell Randolph about Trivett's lynching, when they saw fit.

From behind the cabin, through a fluttering army of hens and chicks, burst Randolph's three sisters. "Mother Hart," they called in unison, over the din.

"Since when are you wearing your Sunday dresses for play?" was the first thing out of her mouth, and no sooner had she finished than Wenda, the middle girl, buried her face in her sister's chest and cried, "But we're having a birthday party for Ma's new baby."

Fletch put a gentle hand on Mother's arm. "You sure you don't want me to get Promise?"

The cabin door opened and closed with the exaggerated caution one used after a beloved had just died. The sweep of her free hand hushed her son.

"Thought I told you to play quiet, till I rang the bell," Thaddeus said to the children as he trudged down the steps toward Mother Hart. His eyes were rimmed in red, the lines around his serious mouth deeper, more tired than usual. "Cornelia was up all the night. First, she wanted to walk, then..." he turned toward the chairs "...she sat outside, while I rubbed her feet and sang to her. When she told me to put the chairs back, my heart got to racing. Then she had me bring them down again. She wasn't like this with our other babies."

Mother Hart eyed the bloodstains on his shirt. "What's happened?"

He looked down at his chest. "Oh, that..." he stammered. "Cornelia...she was twitching this way and that..." He sniffled. "...and I was so tired, and the knife was so dull...only thing it pierced was..." He raised his finger with its angry gash. "I was rushing to slice peaches for Cornelia to suck on."

Mother Hart's sigh turned into a whistle. "That's better than what I thought you were getting around to." She patted the back of Fletch's hand, and gently removed it from her arm. "After I check on Cornelia, I'll brew my best tea. Cornelia, the baby, Thaddeus' finger, everything, and everyone are going to be fine." She borrowed the mantra she'd relied on as her boys were growing up, and revived it with the force of her voice. The expression Fletch had worn after his father's death, when he asked if they were going to be hung, too, melted from his face. "Make sure Thaddeus drinks his tea, you understand, Fletch?" He nodded same as he would any other day, but there was no getting past his scrutiny. Not when she was talking this fast.

She turned towards the children. "Lilly, go get overalls for you and your sisters."

"But Ma doesn't want us inside."

"'Us' is not going inside, you are."

She pulled the drawstring on her birthing bag tight enough to keep its contents from spilling, and slipped it over her arm. The stained deerskin bag nudged her thigh just as Trivett had when he was small. For a moment, his sweaty little boy smell filled her nostrils. She breathed deeply, then eased his spirit by assuring it, "There's a little one coming to fill your space."

The cabin, with its large gathering room and two bedrooms, resembled hers. The table, to which Thaddeus had added a section each time another baby was born, filled the center of the room. Wild flowers bunched in a spoutless pitcher dropped their petals on the frayed yellow tablecloth. On the cook stove, a simmering kettle gave off mare's tails of steam that floated over the counter, where a pile of hacked peach pits rested by Thaddeus' knife.

Pale muslin light shone through the curtains by Cornelia and Thaddeus' bed. Thaddeus had built their lumpy nest with sturdy side rails and, in each corner, smooth stumped posts that were taller where they rested their heads, and shorter at the tail of their narrow mattress. At Cornelia's request, he shaped a foot board, rounding it into two gentle hills, a hip's width apart. Soon, she would position the soles of her feet on the hills, and push their baby through that valley into Mother Hart's hands. Waiting by the window, the rocking cradle with the half-moon runners Thaddeus had carved. A tiny quilt, made with leftover fabric from the dresses Cornelia had sewn for the white ladies in town, had been tucked around a small feathery mattress.

"Don't know as it'll be much longer, Phua," a weary voice said from the bed. Mother Hart smiled; Cornelia was one of the few who called her by the name her mother had given her.

The front door creaked open. Rooting sounds came from the next room. Cornelia lifted her damp head from her pillow. "I told Thaddeus to keep the children outdoors."

Mother Hart stuffed a worn edge under the braided rug, and went into the next room. "Got all three pairs of overalls, Lilly?"

Lilly raised her denim-filled arms. "Tell Mama we're going to make ash cakes for the party."

"That's a good child." The children's bedroom had small beds built out from the walls, one above the other, two on one side, two on the other, with room for two more on the inside wall. A hand-sewn doll with one missing leg fell from beneath Lilly's arm. Mother picked it up. "Oh, that's for Mama to hold until she gets her new baby."

"I'll be sure to give it to her," Mother said, setting the doll by her birthing bag. Lilly skipped across the porch, singing,

"No, sir," to her father's question about having seen her mother.

Mother Hart wrapped a dishcloth around the handle of the iron kettle, and lifted it from the back of the stove. Steam drifted toward the open window over the sink, and coated the cold pump with a rash of tears. She wished she'd thanked Lilly for setting the water to boil. Wished she'd reassured Thaddeus about Cornelia. It wasn't like her to be so thoughtless. She filled the cups with water and added fifteen drops of St. John's wort to one. Later, if Cornelia's pain demanded it, she'd add a few drops of skullcap. In a separate cup, she swirled dried peach leaves for Cornelia's favorite tea, and recited a favorite passage from the Bible: "...the leaves of the trees were for the healing of the midwife." She glanced out the open window to see if anyone had heard her mistake, then corrected the passage: "...the leaves of the trees were for the healing of nations." *Trivett's death is hobbling your memory*, a voice from deep within her cautioned.

She'd gotten on after her husband's murder, but this time, she doubted she'd be able to move forward, not after having lost the little boy they'd adopted. She'd failed her husband's trust when she failed to protect their children, and, though Trivett was a grown man, she'd failed him, too. It wasn't until she heard Fletch's soft voice that she remembered she'd promised to make the men tea. She dropped a slice of ginger into their cups, and poured one for herself; she could use some soothing, too.

Thaddeus and Fletch sat facing one another at the bottom of the stairs, a checkerboard balanced on their knees. The sun shone in Thaddeus' eyes, and when he looked up at her, his scowl increased her edginess. Was he wishing he'd gone for Promise instead of her? She'd never told him, she cherished the confidence he placed in her, and that it enhanced her ability to heal. Sensing his doubt, she wondered if Fletch knew her mind better than she; perhaps she had been mistaken to come; during a birth, a midwife's thoughts ought to be committed to the living, never the dead.

"How's Cornelia?" Thaddeus asked, sloshing water from the two half-filled cups onto his hands. His squinting eyes brimmed with suspicion.

"Fletch, get my ax from the wagon."

The wooden checkers scattered.

"You sure Cornelia's all right?" Thaddeus fretted.

She summoned her surest voice. "She will be."

When Mother returned, Cornelia was kneeling by the bed, back arched, face pressed to the mattress. The babe hung low inside her. Mother set St. John's wort tea to the left, and peach tea to the right on the night table. She bent aside Cornelia, and slipped the ax out from under her elbow. "I'm gonna ease the pressure."

Cornelia winced and looked away. "Hurry."

A groan and a hollow sound followed the thud of the ax scraping across the floorboards. An ax under the bed cuts the pain of birthing. And of grief.

Mother straddled Cornelia's bare legs and slid her hands down her muscular back, over her once-indented waist to the fleshy round of her hips. She'd taught Cornelia to take charge of her pain, to work it by rocking her hips, panting softly and whispering after every breath. "Conversing with the pain eases it into behaving," Cornelia said, once she'd relaxed.

I believed that once but not any more, Mother Hart thought, massaging the tightness knotting her forehead. Others, who'd begged her to stop the agony of their womanhood being forced wider than they imagined possible, were able to concentrate once she'd convinced them of the power of their pain: "Without it, you'd abandon the task nature set out for you to do." Her words held true, if the hurt was lightening quick and no bigger than a teardrop; when it wasn't, she drowned their pain with potent herb teas. The same ones she drank to keep memories of her husband's death from hammering at her heart. And her pain? That had stretched her so far, if much more time passed, she feared it would slide her inside out, render her incapable of attending to the one most important job she had yet to complete.

Cornelia groaned. "This one's giving me trouble, Phua. This baby's wrong, I can feel it."

"You need the slop pot before you settle?"

Cornelia nodded. Mother fetched the enamel pot from beneath the night table. "Just put it on the floor," Cornelia said.

When she finished peeing, Cornelia crawled to the foot of the bed and settled her backside on the clean muslin sheets she'd put down for this very purpose. Mother propped Cornelia's neck and shoulders with pillows. When she'd made Cornelia as comfortable as any woman in the birthing way could be, she washed her hands in the tub at the foot of the bed. "We'll use curly dock oil to help that child slide out easy."

She rubbed the deep yellow oil around her close-cut nails, over her fingers and palms. When they were soft as new butter, she scooped a hint more and massaged it in small firm circles over Cornelia's opening.

"That's nice, Phua, so nice. You gonna tell me the Bible story about the midwives, like you always do?" Seconds later, her face twisted with pain. Mother Hart pushed herself up from her knees, gathered her skirt, and joined Cornelia, lying there as God, with Thaddeus' help, had created her—darkened nipples in swollen breasts resting on her rounded belly, the mark of her connection with her own mother flattened into a reminder of what once was. She held a lavender compress to Cornelia's forehead, and waited until the pain had done its work. When it had passed, she returned to the foot of the bed.

With her thoughts creeping one over the other, Mother Hart had difficulty recalling the tale Cornelia wanted to hear, so she pieced together a new one:

"The King of Egypt had lived in exile for over twenty years, and when he finally returned, he brought with him a meanness the likes of which the Hebrews had almost forgotten. Now the King disliked these people, thought of them as slaves who caused all his troubles. While it wasn't his habit to speak directly with them, particularly the women, he summoned two Hebrew midwives, Sephora and Phua, to his chambers. He told them when it came time for a Hebrew woman to give birth, they were to feed the girl babies, and lynch the boys."

Cornelia lifted her head, her face scribbled with worry.

"Another pain, Cornelia?"

"I don't recall the king saying that," she murmured, dropping back into her flattened pillow.

"Let's hope you never do." Mother plumped the pillow, then continued: "These midwives told the King that Hebrew mothers were unlike the Egyptian ladies. 'Hebrew mothers,' Sephora said, 'are skilled at birthing, and do so without waiting for Phua and me to arrive.' That made sense to the King. 'Women who have the ability to cross the desert would surely do this themselves. I must think of another plan,' he said. Phua took a potion from her sack and poured it into the King's goblet. "This drink discerns the weak from the truly powerful, and makes those who are great, greater." The King drank greedily. "It is searing my throat," were the last words to escape his lips. And so, the clever midwives silenced the King's cruelest weapon, and Hebrew boy babies grew into the men who would later defeat the King's armies."

"Aaahh." The next pain overpowered Cornelia. Mother Hart climbed on the bed and worked her legs under Cornelia's shoulders. Cornelia puffed her cheeks, forced her peachy breath out, slowly at first, then, as the pain worsened, in quick little bellows. When it was over, she rested her head against

Mother. Cornelia's hair, freed from the knot atop her head, covered Mother's chest with damp black waves, just as her husband's had when men in white robes dropped his limp body into her arms. She slid her hands along Cornelia's narrow face, humming same as she'd done for her husband. His tortures had left his handsome face like Cornelia's, wet and contorted. She stroked Cornelia's damp cheeks, hummed a little more, then stroked and hummed some more. No matter how sweetly she hummed or how fast she stroked, there was no bringing her husband back; this she knew, and though her mind commanded her hands to stop stroking, they only moved faster.

"Phua, enough!" Cornelia looked up, her brown eyelashes touching her eyebrows, her face, a muddy mix of annoyance and strain suddenly lightened with recognition. "I've lost my water, Phua. I want to push!" Her gaze became fixed. She'd taken to concentrating.

Mother scrambled off the bed, tugged her skirt into place, and searched her birthing bag. Where had she put her twine? Why hadn't she checked her bag like she always did before leaving her house? She tossed her notebook, scissors, bandages, towels, and soap, aside. *My twine's gone missing*, she thought, lifting her scissors and dropping them, doing the same with each of the other things, and sifting through them once more.

She ran to the front door, yanked it open, and hollered, "Fletcher, baby's coming, and I can't find the twine to tie it off with. Look in the wagon. Hurry!" then slammed the door.

Cornelia's screaming ended with a grunt each time she pushed. Having misplaced the twine was all Mother Hart could think about. "What will the King say when he hears the midwife lost her twine?" she mumbled. "He can't hang baby boys if he doesn't have his twine," she announced with a maniacal grin.

Cornelia had stopped pushing, and was panting. "Phua, what's the matter? What's happening to you?" Her worried voice, her woman's smells brought Mother back.

She peered at Cornelia's opening. There, waiting to get out, not a soft wet head, but skin that had no business showing itself first. Mother Hart splashed water over her hands, and scrubbed them good. "With this water, I cleanse my thoughts of demons," she prayed, dipping her hands into the basin, and bringing them up to dry. She rubbed her fingers with oil, and slid them between Cornelia and the baby. Though its slippery sack formed a thin barrier between her and its arm, the smallest of fingertips wiggled within her grasp. "It's spreading my bones apart!" cried Cornelia.

Extending the baby's arm, Mother eased the hand through its satiny caul, past its head, and out into the world. Cornelia pushed. The back of the shoulder followed with the head tucked close, and the little body slipped into Mother's large waiting hands. The boy child glistened in the afternoon light, flopped silently until, struck by the change he'd just endured, wailed. Mucus drained from his nose and mouth as she placed him, attached by his throbbing cord, face down on his mother's breast. At this, his first encounter with the touch of another human, the poor babe flinched. And why shouldn't he? The blue splotch on his behind, a mere spill of God's ink, was a reminder to all dark babies that they were like his own son, condemned to be different from the start. *A cruel joke*, thought Mother, as if between now and the next few hours, weeks, months or years—whenever that mark disappeared—the infant's life wouldn't be complicated enough.

Cornelia counted his fingers and toes, then ran her fingertip over his sweet brown forehead, pushed his damp down this way and that, and, at last, covered his face with teary soft kisses.

The curls of his pearly gray cord would pulse a few minutes more. It smelled of iron, like the earth during a spring rain. Water sloshed in the basin as Mother cleaned Cornelia, who hadn't torn an inch, then the baby. Mother hummed the same lullaby she'd hummed for her little boys, two of her own, and Trivett, the one God sent her to care for. She swallowed hard, and folded one hand over the other to keep them from shaking.

"Rest, both of you," she said, lowering the sheet over them, and leaving to answer the knock on the door. Through the haze of the screen, she eyed the twine in Fletch's palm. "Tell William Hart he has another son," she told him, repeating the words her own mother had called out after Fletch had been born.

Fletch winced. "Mam? You feeling poorly again?"

The shock on her son's face brought her words back in all their oddity. "Can't help it if the past drops in at a time like this, now can I?" She stroked his chin, took the sack from his hand and added, "I'm fine, truly."

By now, Thaddeus had set the checker board aside, and was hugging his children. "What will you name your fine boy?" she asked.

"Cornelia and I...we were thinking of Whittling."

"Whittling," she repeated. "Because he looks like a shaving that escaped the hanging tree." She took in Thaddeus' shock, then turned to close the door. "Barbed talk isn't like her. Something has nettled her mind," she overheard him say. Much to her relief, the kind man understood.

She paused by the bed: the baby had fallen asleep, and Cornelia was concentrating. "Good," Mother murmured, pushing the curtains aside and tossing the bloody water from the basin out the window. Then she slipped the basin under Cornelia. Within minutes, the dark red bumps of the second birth quivered against the white enamel. Mother checked to make sure everything had been emptied.

After a few minutes, the cord went still. She lowered it into the basin, and placed it alongside the baby. She tied the twine into a slipknot, eased it close to the baby, and prayed silently: *Let this be the only rope you'll ever know.* With Cornelia's other babies, Mother Hart had waited a full hour for the second birth to stop pulsing before separating it. Today, she cut this baby free.

Thaddeus had just returned the chairs to the porch. A small peach tree in a bucket waited by a fresh hole, where it would be planted with the afterbirth in hopes Whittling would never know hunger. "Is this what you're waiting for?" Mother asked, handing Thaddeus the basin. The happy sound of the children scurrying into the cabin after their father was her answer.

Fletch took the basin and set it on the chair. "I do believe Whittling has led me to a decision I've been avoiding," she told him.

"Have you made yourself a promise, Mam?"

"I have, Fletcher William, I have."

He leaned toward her. "Are you going to tell me what it is?"

A glimmer of happiness, the likes of which she hadn't observed since his father had died, shone in her son's gentle eyes. His face glowed, as though he pictured her engaged in a worthwhile deed, an act that would change them all for the better. He'd guessed right and wrong. She closed her eyes and shook her head; no was how she answered his question. No mother would divulge a promise such as hers.

Thaddeus and Lilly came out of the cabin, he wearing a soft smile, carrying Mother's belongings, Lilly concentrating on the contents of the small basket pressed to her chest. "Mama says we need to save our ash cakes till Whittling grows his teeth."

"I agree with your mama. How's Cornelia?" Mother asked Thaddeus.

"She told me what you done for her and our baby. I'm grateful, Phua." He nodded to Lilly, who handed her the basket.

"No need to pay me. You and Cornelia are like family." Mother counted five speckled eggs in a bed of hay.

"T'ain't much, one for each baby. I'd give you more, if I had 'em to give."

"Five should make a fine supper."

The baby started crying, a strong, healthy sound. Thaddeus listened, and as he did, handed the birthing bag to Fletch, and the ax to Mother Hart. "You'll be needing this," he said, as though he'd gleaned the murderous nature of her promise.

She caught the startled recognition in Fletch's eyes, and averted hers. "Go Thaddeus, see to your family."

While Fletch hitched the mule to the wagon, Mother hoisted herself onto the seat, positioned the ax under her foot, arranged her skirt, and settled the basket in her lap. Fatigue, heavier than a rain-drenched cloak, settled on her. She sighed; she'd set out to be strong, and that's what she'd done. Barely. As Fletch climbed up beside her, she prayed her sanity would serve her until she fulfilled her vengeful promise. She wedged the basket between her hip and the side of the seat farthest from her son, where he wouldn't see two of her eggs lay broken and oozing.

WHERE YOU BEGIN

My mother bore down on the stubby handle of her serrated knife and disconnected the wingtip from a raw chicken breast. Though it was unusually warm for April, the flare of her nostrils and crunch of the bones made me shiver. "What are you doing?" I asked, and plopped my schoolbooks on the chair. The gray vinyl went whoosh, and Dad's bomb shelter plans skittered to her feet.

"No matter how I arrange these, the wings always touch the broiler. This way nothing gets burned." She jammed the breast in with the others, seemed strangely satisfied.

"Why don't you move the oven rack away from the broiler?"

She shook her head, said I didn't understand. She was right. She leaned against the kitchen counter, and sank her knife into another breast, dividing the sternum in two; its tiny bones exploded.

Her short auburn hair was standing on end. Her tan blouse stuck to her slim back, and when she turned around, dirt-streaks lined the front of her purple pedal pushers. "How was your day, Donna?" she asked, her glasses on the tip of her perfectly shaped nose.

"I stopped at the store, and asked Roger to my senior prom." I slipped my sandy hair behind my ear, away from my face without having to be told.

"I take it Roger said 'yes.'" She suspended her knife in mid-air while she read my smile. "Just think, Mitchell's is the biggest store in Hartford, and Roger Mitchell is my daughter's prom date. Your father will be so proud." Her tone lilted with sarcasm. Her breath smelled of scotch.

"Why does Mrs. Mitchell's store have to come up whenever I mention Roger?" I hoped she wouldn't remind me that years before I started working part-time for Helena Snag-the-Boys Mitchell, she and my mother had been best friends.

My mother glanced toward the hall closet where she'd stored the knit dresses and suits she'd once tried to sell to our neighbors. Always the entrepreneur, when this scheme failed, she tried the plastic containers you have to burp before settling into her latest venture, Fabulous Foundations, an exclusive line of ladies underwear. Now the closet brimmed with boxes marked Control Zipper Hi-Rises, Tummy Shapers, Body Briefs, and Front-Closing Long Lines. I imagined her bragging about Roger Mitchell to her customers and the beehived members of her social clubs. The ones my father and I detested.

"You ever think how lucky you are to go out with Roger? After all, he meets hundreds of girls at the store, but he chose you."

Chose for what? I scowled. "I like Daddy's analysis better—Roger's lucky I agreed to go out with him."

"I could faint every time you say that. If only you'd known your father when we were dating. He did the choosing while being a lady meant I had to wait to be chosen." She picked up a glass from the counter, seemed surprised it was empty.

"But that's changing, Mom. I'm the one who asked Roger to my prom. Wasn't that the point of sending me to a girls' academy?" I flashed my onyx and gold class ring with the inscription, To Learn, Lead and Have Vision.

She arched her left eyebrow. "Don't forget, I graduated from Laurel Academy, too. And this afternoon, my vision was full of the rose bushes your father bought and never planted." She massaged her lower back. "Will you help me fix dinner? Your father has a meeting tonight. He wants to eat early." She sounded tired like she always did when she talked about my father.

Our narrow kitchen had one small counter by the sink and two wall cabinets, one in the corner by the harvest gold stove, and the other between the stove and the matching refrigerator. I squeezed in next to my mother to wash my hands. The heat radiating from her body penetrated my A-line uniform skirt. I usually change into cutoffs, but that wasn't the clothing item on my mind. "Mom, I've decided what kind of dress I want for the prom."

She set her knife down, and wiped the perspiration from her forehead. She was smiling now, and I could feel my smile becoming dreamy as I described a fitted sheath beneath a flowing lace gown.

"Sounds pretty. Simple yet elegant," she said, cocking her head to one side, the way she did when she was deciding on an undergarment for a customer.

The following Saturday, I was scheduled to work at Mitchell's. I'd planned to start shopping for my gown during my lunch hour, and assumed my mother would join me as she usually did. But like most things I counted on my mother for, it didn't work out. Even though her gourmet club wouldn't arrive until that evening, its preparations topped her list of things to do. Four couples decked in gowns and suits would be coming to our house for their monthly dinner. Everything from floors to food had to be perfect.

I punched my time card, and scurried toward the salesladies in Women's Swimsuits. They stood in a circle, hands by their corseted sides, waiting for the morning department meeting to start. When they saw me, their lips melted into lopsided smiles—my prom date had taken on huge proportions.

The buyer, a motherly woman with dark braids pinned at the base of her head approached me. "New dress, Mrs. Barton?" She blushed, looked down at the well-tailored seams outlining her lumpy figure, and motioned for me to hurry.

"We have a surprise for you," she said in her breathless little-girl voice as she guided me into the circle.

The ladies tittered, cast knowing looks at one another, then at me. I gulped. "Today's not my birthday," I said, looking for the telltale box of Danish pastry from the fifth floor bakery.

"This is more exciting." Mrs. Barton nodded at Tall Eddie, the stock man, who wheeled a rolling rack draped in brown canvas into the middle of the circle.

"New merchandise?" I asked, knowing bathing suits came in small, flat boxes.

"When we heard about your prom date..." Giggling interrupted Mrs. Barton as she switched to her this-is-an-important-announcement voice. "...I contacted the buyer in Women's Evening Wear, and asked her to put aside her latest shipment of size ten gowns." Tall Eddie removed the canvas curtain. In what seemed to be choreographed movements, each saleslady lifted a gown, and held it up. I gasped at the rich satins, beaded bodices and lace.

"Quick, try them on before the store opens," Mrs. Barton said. The plastic bags protecting the gowns rustled as the ladies swooped me into the fitting rooms.

A bevy of hands lifted my cardigan from my shoulders, unzipped my dress, and guided me into the first of many gowns. I promenaded onto the sales floor, my neck long, spine straight, and wrists extended like I'd seen the models do during the spring fashion show. Mrs. Barton, the ladies, and Tall Eddie beamed at my little princess routine. You'd think as the only child, I would have been accustomed to this kind of attention, but I wasn't. I lapped it up like the gift of cool water to a stray dog on a hot day.

The last one. Everyone agreed that the bare-shouldered look was the most flattering, but it was the way Tall Eddie's eyes sparkled that made me decide on that last dress. It was the prettiest. And the most expensive. I called my mother to get her permission to charge it to her account.

"Sorry, Mom, I didn't realize the cleaning lady was there. Go ahead, answer the door." She dropped the phone, letting it bang against the wall. She reeled off a list of chores that would make the house look 'extra special.' The delay gave me time to figure out my employee discount: fifteen percent of one hundred and twenty-five dollars.

My mother returned, and before I could get to the price said, "Sure, put it on my charge account. Your father will pay for it." I felt like another chore that had just been crossed off.

I entertained the thought of describing my dress detail by lousy detail, just to keep her on the phone. But I couldn't. "Thanks, I'll do that," I said, real casual like. I turned to the salesladies gathered around me, and gave them the thumbs up sign. They whirled on their sensible heels, and made silent clapping gestures.

Tall Eddie was getting ready to return the gowns to the seventh floor when Mrs. Mitchell appeared from the other side of a rack of bikinis. She'd come downstairs from her penthouse on the tenth floor, and was making her rounds to each department. As usual, she wore a fresh corsage of white carnations, and her graying hair had been neatly tucked into a French twist with spit curls arcing on either side of her forehead. These things had never meant much, but today, I found them comforting.

Mrs. Mitchell gave me a gentle hug. "I hear Roger gets to bring the prettiest girl at Laurel Academy to her prom."

Before I could say anything, Mrs. Barton bustled from the back room, and pointed to my gown, which she'd draped over her arm. "Look at what she's buying. Such a sense of style...a buyer in the making, don't you think?"

Mrs. Mitchell lifted the strapless gown. "It's perfect, Donna." She glanced at Tall Eddie, leaned over, and whispered in my ear. "Have you thought about the undergarment you'll need with this?" I was about to explain that my mother owned Fabulous Foundations when she said, "Tell Mrs. Finley, in Lingerie, I sent you."

"I will, thank you." And I would. I'd have to. My stomach gurgled. I imagined Mrs. Mitchell on one end of a strapless bra tugging so hard her fingers turned pink, while my mother pulled on the other end until the elastic bodice stretched hideously out-of-shape. I excused myself, and hurried to the ladies room.

That evening, I opened the front door to our sparkling house, expecting to find my mother fussing over the tarnished silverware and chipped goblets that 'just wouldn't do' for her friends. In its place, were delicious aromas and a hushed calm.

Tony Bennett crooned, "I wanna be around to pick up the pieces…" I tiptoed with my garment bag into the kitchen.

My mother swayed beneath her seersucker housecoat. She jutted her pink and green roller-dotted head over the stove, and sampled a spoonful of sauce. "Um…cooking with brandy brings out the best in everything," she said, and leaned her cheek into my kiss.

I glared at her half-empty glass of amber liquid. You mean everyone, I wanted to say.

She glanced at my bag, and smiled. "That's your gown? Go, put it on."

I started to tell her about Mrs. Mitchell, then hesitated, knowing she'd get upset. She downed a mouthful of brandy, and that did it—I couldn't stop myself. "I need to buy a strapless bra, and Roger's mother gave me the name of her personal saleslady, said she'd be a big help."

"Did you tell her your mother specializes in foundations?" She sounded catty and injured at the same time.

I turned to go up the back stairway to my bedroom. I was ashamed at my meanness, and needed to escape before I spilled my guts about how good it felt to have someone take care of me for a change. "I'll be down in a second," I said, catching my foot on the garment bag, and almost stumbling on the step.

My mother eyed the wall clock. "I haven't finished the hors d'oeuvres yet. How about showing me your dress after my guests leave?"

I knew what that meant. Tomorrow. Maybe. Depending on how hung over she'd be.

As I started up the stairs, my father's chair creaked in his third floor study. My footsteps echoed in the narrow stairwell that led to what he called his "inner sanctum."

"Hi, Daddy." He leaned forward, shoulders hunched, scissors in hand, about to clip an old news article for his history scrapbook. Copies of *The Hartford Times* and *The Courant* were stacked on his desk. "Day Eleven...Cuban Missile Crisis," the headline from last fall's paper topped the pile.

"How's my girl?" He took off his tortoise shell glasses, leaned back, and stretched out his long legs. The springs in his chair squealed. Daddy hadn't yet changed out of his gray suit trousers and wingtips. I smiled. Shoes are what first attracted me to Roger, who wore the same style. They were well built, good-looking, and reliable. The type an honest man would wear.

"Your mother tells me you're mastering the art of spending my hard-earned money." He pushed his sandy hair from his eyes, and motioned me toward him. "Let's see what you bought." He leaned forward, absentmindedly fingering an article about the Vietnam War. We both adored President Kennedy, and spent many dinner conversations arguing the fine points of containment and domino theory with my mother, who made no secret of wishing Nixon had won the election.

I pressed the lace-covered sheath to my chest and twirled around.

"Gorgeous."

"That's what Mrs. Mitchell said." I told him about my morning at work. He listened, his brown eyes fixed on mine.

"I sold Mr. Mitchell his life insurance policy, you know. It made Mrs. Mitchell a fabulously wealthy woman."

"You tell me that every time I mention the store."

He smiled. "That's in case you've forgotten. Mrs. Mitchell's a terrific lady. She and I were in the same English class. She won the Golden Pen Award that year for a story she wrote about a mare that adopted the jenny-foal of a dying donkey. She must think a lot of you. I'll have to stop in and thank her."

"You make her sound like a saint."

He shrugged. "I took her to my senior prom, you know."

"No, I didn't know." For a moment, neither of us said a word. My father's chair creaked as he turned toward the window, a happy expression on his weary face. I felt as though I was intruding. I put my hands on my hips and took a deep breath. "You took Mom's best friend to your prom? What did Mom have to say about that?"

"She didn't care, she was dating Mitch at the time."

"Mitch?"

"Mr. Mitchell."

"She never told me that. What happened?"

"His family wanted someone with a higher pedigree, and her family wanted someone with a healthier bank account." He wore a sheepish expression that irked the hell out of me, almost made me forget the reason I'd tromped upstairs. I pictured my mother's gourmet friends. "Mom seemed awfully relaxed when I came in. She's usually a nervous wreck before one of her parties. Don't you think you should check on her?"

"She's fine, Donna. Really." I shot him a skeptical look. Because she's been drinking, I wanted to say, but my father didn't want to hear it. He preferred actuarial tables that predicted how much your next of kin would inherit if you died today versus five years from today, to anything he didn't know what to do about. "If we could combine those figures with what we know about history, we could predict the future," he liked to say. I glanced at the Vietnam article in his hand; it was my mother who needed containment.

The next day, my mother shuffled back and forth to the bathroom, her housecoat half unbuttoned, her hand over her mouth. The gagging as she arched over the toilet made me gag, too. I held my breath and flushed, wiped her face with a cool washcloth, and guided her back to her bed. After she'd fallen asleep, I crammed my gown in the back of my closet, and spent the afternoon on the third floor with my father.

From then on, I avoided talking about Mrs. Mitchell or the store, and I didn't dare ask my mother about the strapless bra she'd promised me, although I was anxious to try it on with my gown. Mrs. Finley in Lingerie had warned me about the cut of the bra not matching the cut of the dress. "The brassiere might stick out around the bust line of your gown, and that would be embarrassing, wouldn't it? Even though both garments belong to the same person, you can't assume they're going to fit well together."

She was so right. My mother had stopped asking me about school or work. She never mentioned the prom, and disappeared whenever Roger came over. When I complained to my father, he said it sounded like a classic Cold War stand-off, like the ones Kennedy and Khrushchev got in to. I asked him how long it would last; he had no idea.

But my mother seemed to know she was making me uneasy, and delighted in pointing out the acne on my face. "Nerves getting to you, dear?" she asked.

"Absolutely, but only because I haven't heard from any colleges yet."

When I bemoaned the absence of mail addressed to me, my mother asked, "What makes my baby bird in such a rush to leave her nest?" My father consoled me with, "No college admissions committee would reject a young woman who washes her hair every night."

Mrs. Mitchell seemed to understand. She stopped in the swimwear department whenever she was on the fourth floor. Always cheery and polite, she never asked if I'd heard anything from Cornell, Columbia, or Northeastern, even though she'd written letters of recommendation for me. Rather, she waited until I told her I still hadn't heard a thing. "The colleges and universities are notoriously late with their acceptances this year. They've been inundated with applications. Draft dodgers, you know. Don't worry, yours will stand out against the others." She noticed my blue bag, sealed with a neat line of staples the store security officer had pounded into place. "How did you do with Mrs. Finley?"

I held up the bag with its Mitchell's logo prominently displayed. "Right in here. It's like having a second skin—soft and feminine—it fits perfectly. I can't wait to wear it." I didn't like lying, but I'd checked my mother's orders to see if she placed one for a strapless bra my size. She hadn't. Armed with my father's words, "History truly repeats itself," I decided my mother had no intention of helping me, and that I'd wind up wearing the bra Mrs. Finley had fitted me for. Then I wouldn't be lying.

Mrs. Mitchell smiled knowingly. Dainty lines framed her speckled brown eyes. I wanted to follow her to her penthouse, beg her to adopt me. I caught myself thinking more of her than Roger, and suspected she was the reason I was dating him.

That and the attention he brought me at work. "Have you decided how you're going to have your hair styled?" one of the salesladies asked as she scurried toward a customer. "Don't forget, tell Roger you'll need a wrist courage," said another. Even Tall Eddie wanted to know if Mrs. Mitchell's chauffeur would drive us to the prom.

But it was Roger's announcement that surprised me most. "My mother's hired the store photographer to take pictures of us," he said the week before the prom. We'd just seen *The Birds,* and were at the Farmshop in West Hartford, waiting for the "take-out queen" to heap my favorite, peppermint ice cream, on a sugar cone. I was so shocked, I forgot to remind Roger I wanted chocolate jimmies.

"Why can't she use the flash camera you gave her for Christmas? The one my father helped you pick out?" My words hit me like a runaway freight train. My father had brought Roger to an expensive camera shop, bought him lunch, then made a big deal out of their afternoon together as if Roger was someone special. What if it wasn't Roger my father wanted to connect with? He'd stayed in contact with Roger's mother, sold her insurance, and spent a lot of time helping her collect on her husband's policy. He'd even planned to thank her for taking an interest in me. Was it that simple? I didn't think so.

I stood inches from Roger's freckled red chin. He was unbuttoning the back pocket of his chinos, and would, any second now, be digging for his wallet. I followed his long slender pant leg to his cuff, expecting to see his reassuring wingtips. Instead, he wore rust-colored penny loafers with thick crinkled soles. I turned away, upset.

"In case you haven't noticed, my mother's employees do everything for her. I know, I'm one of them." Rubber-sole Man peered down at me, his Springer Spaniel face contorted as if it pained him to burst my Mrs. Mitchell, a.k.a. fairy godmother, bubble. But it wasn't her bubble that was dripping a slippery film; it was my father's. I bit my lip to keep from crying.

"That's ridiculous, no one's as competent as your mother."

"Think about it. She has a cook, a housekeeper, a chauffeur, and she pays Mrs. Barton extra to do her shopping. Her florist pins her corsage on every morning before she meets with her personal secretary. Who did you think wrote your college recommendations?" His eyes popped—he'd unleashed a family secret.

"Here you go, sir." The bosomy waitress planted her elbows on the counter, a napkin-wrapped cone in each fist. Roger pivoted like a garden gate between the waitress and me. Chocolate, double scoop for him. Peppermint, no jimmies for me.

Figures, I thought and sunk my teeth into the green and pink speckled hardness. A wedge of peppermint candy jammed between my teeth, making them ache. I couldn't decide which hurt most—the cold jolt ricocheting through my head, or my suspicion that my father had never stopped seeing Snag-the-Boys-Mitchell.

"You okay?" Roger asked, smacking his lips as he lapped his ice cream. He slipped his arm around my waist, and chomped on a mouthful of sugar cone.

I forced myself to swallow. "You sure your mother didn't write my letters?"

"Not in a million years. She says if it hadn't been for your father, she would have flunked English."

My father's reminiscences about Mrs. Mitchell's story danced like cannibals around a boiling cauldron. Just who was being cooked, I wasn't sure. "My father would never let your mother pass his story in as hers." Roger stared at me, stupid and befuddled. I glared at him, then at his shoes. It was the second time in the last twenty minutes I hated Roger Mitchell.

I stopped visiting my father on the third floor. When he came down, I no longer made eye contact, and I sure as hell didn't talk with him about my mother. I consoled myself by listing all the things I'd managed to do without anyone's mother. I'd pressed my gown, and hung it on the back of my closet door. Arranged my garter belt and stockings on my bed next to the shoes I'd dyed to match the powder blue ribbon along the bodice of my gown. I draped my mother's lacey shawl beside my shoes. She probably didn't remember buying it, much less my not having returned it after last year's dance. At least I hoped so. I planned on carrying it in case prom night turned chilly.

I peered into my full-length mirror. My mother's seersucker bathrobe fit more snugly on me than on her. Unlike mine, it buttoned up the front, and, after bathing, I lifted it from its hook behind the bathroom door, and slipped it around me so I wouldn't disturb the French curls Mrs. Mitchell's beautician had pinned in place. I picked at the wispy tendrils of hair; they bounced spring-like, and returned to their original position, unscathed.

Outside, beneath my bedroom window, my mother yanked furiously at the weeds in my father's garden. "I asked her to tidy the rose bed so I could take your picture there," my father had said moments earlier as he stood in the kitchen squirreling packages of film into his pockets. Now that I thought he was having an affair, his soft boyish voice seemed put on, innocent to a fault. I think my mother knew, too. Why else would she drink?

It was after six o'clock. Roger would be here at six-thirty, and my strapless bra was still hidden in the back of my closet. I didn't want it on my bed in case my mother barged in. In case she decided she'd left herself out of her only daughter's only senior prom long enough. I planned to put it on last, then slip quickly into my gown. I didn't want a scene; I wanted an uneventful escape.

I unbuttoned the bathrobe, and fastened my garter belt around my hips, then sat on my bed, gathered one of my stockings into a tidy mound of nylon, and slipped it over my toe, knee, up my thigh, and beneath a shiny clasp. I flexed my knee to make sure I'd left enough play in the stocking. There's nothing quite as startling as the breech you feel when you pop a runner that unravels those nylon fibers so fast you lose track of where the damage ends and you begin.

The back door slammed. My mother trudged up the steps. As she moved down the hallway so did the ice in her glass. First, with a resigned rhythmic clunking, then whirling faster, louder, until I thought her glass would shatter. She stopped outside my door. I held my breath, didn't move. When she clattered into her bedroom, I rushed to get my other stocking on, and was about to finish dressing when the door burst open.

"You probably thought I forgot this," my mother said. Dangling between her soil-stained thumb and index finger was a white birdcage-like object. She plunked it on my bureau. It teetered for a moment, then stood bolt upright.

"What is it?"

"It's the strapless bra I told you about. I wore it the day your father and I were married."

I approached it with caution. "That's not a bra, it's a harness." It ran about eighteen inches from top to bottom, with French seams that shrouded five pairs of stays, long bones, like my grandmother used in her corset. At the bottom, hung four rubber knobs with rusty stocking clasps.

"It's an all in one—bra and garter belt," my mother said. She had a faraway look on her face, like my father's that day in his study, and, like him, seemed to have slipped back to a time when her dreams sparkled with hope.

I ran my fingers over the white stitches that bisected the cups. Their rugged sturdiness was exactly what you might need—if you were going to a jousting match. My mother pushed her bathrobe off my shoulders. It puddled around my ankles. We stared in the mirror at my pale, delicately blue-veined breasts. I was too stunned to be embarrassed.

"You won't need your garter belt, take it off." I did what my mother said, all the while feeling like a little kid. One who'd do anything for her mother.

As she reached to wrap her bra around me, her whiskey-tainted breath floated on the air. My mother had always confused me. Just as I was about to write her off, hate her even, she came through. Kind of. I let her position my breasts in the stiff cups, and held them in place while she hooked me in. Every once in a while, the fabric slipped from her grasp, and she sucked her breath in and whispered, "Oh, no."

"Got it, Mom?" She yanked hard, pulling me toward her, knocking me off balance, then catching me. Her warm hands on my bare shoulders steadied me, and, for a moment, I leaned into her, let her take care of me the way I'd always wanted. Her gentle movements set me upright as if to say, this is the way things are, and this is how you stand tall. When she finished, the stiff stays left me no choice.

My mother wiped her hands on her jeans and slipped my gown over my head, careful not to disturb my curls. Even before she finished zipping, I could see that the top of her bra was going to stick out from under my gown. I looked around for safety pins so I could hide the little wingtips.

I thought of the grimy little holes in my father's wingtips, of my mother hacking at those breasts. No matter which recipe she tried, the chicken always burned. I glanced at my bureau, at the tray beside her wedding picture where I kept my scissors; they weren't there. Even if they had been, I'd never cut her strapless bra. It would have hurt too much.

LYDIA'S FLASH ENLIGHTENMENT

Lydia entered the house to find her husband, Charles, talking on the phone in his study. He'd been running his financial planning business from home for over a year, and had recently located a suitable office space to rent. "Hello dear, I'm back," she called out, thinking he would continue to work as he usually did, without acknowledging her presence. Minutes later, Charles appeared wearing an expression so sweet it made Lydia think he understood she'd returned from the grocery store with renewed determination to be a part of his life.

She smiled. She'd just climbed the kitchen stepladder, and was about to place an armful of canned goods on the top shelf of her pantry, but she stepped down, left the groceries in disarray, and tiptoed across the room to greet Charles. He wore a preoccupied smile, the variety of which she'd hadn't seen in years. The word, "titillated" thrummed in her head.

Curious, Lydia turned toward him. Had he noticed how youthful and bright she appeared one week before her fiftieth birthday? She did feel like the very breath of spring today, full of life, and renewed confidence. Or, had he watched her after this morning's bath, slipping her youthful thighs into the legs of her delicious, Barely-There Thong? Perhaps he was about to invite her for a tryst on the living room sofa in broad daylight? It'd been years...

She placed her mouth on his, her face at an angle over his narrow lips. They intersected in an X. Light and sloppy, their kiss was brief, a disappointing mid-day interlude. For a moment, he looked surprised, pleasantly so, and that pleased her. *I'll have to do that more often*, she promised herself. She was about to return to the pantry, with its purple-red mahogany cabinets, copper counter, and geraniums blooming despite the twenty-two degrees on the other side of the window, when she noticed Charles hadn't moved. He stood by the oak table, his forefinger in mid-air shaped like a question mark.

"Yes, dear?" she said, and waited for him to speak.

Charles scratched his shinny head and hesitated, confused, perhaps, by what had just transpired. His beige cardigan sweater hung from his shoulders, a buttonhole by his neck and a leather button, unfastened at his waistline.

Lydia admired the afternoon light on his ruddy skin, and those bushy eyebrows, arching umbrella-like over his royal blue eyes.

"I was wondering if you had the address for the insurance company," he said, running his foot back and forth over the crushed heel of his loafer. It reminded her of the first time he had asked her for a date, thirty-four years ago.

Her smile fizzled. Determined not to show Charles her disappointment, she responded with what she hoped would be a pleasing tone of voice. "It's in your study, in your Rolodex. Under I." She cringed; she hadn't meant to say the last two words so harshly.

Half-smiling, Charles pivoted toward his study door, then stopped. Lydia caught her breath. *You should have had more confidence in his sensitivities,* she chided herself. He was getting business out of the way in preparation to say something like, "What would I do without you?" or "You're so efficient, and a wonderful lover too."

"I have to send them my new address," he said.

Charles' loafers clicked against her Italian kitchen tiles, and Lydia sighed as she thought of the satisfaction she'd get when she finished putting her groceries away.

THREADS

Joseba should have guessed his sister-in-law would lead with a shot about their having lived together in Barcelona. He'd left himself open when he'd asked Lynn to meet him at his beach house. The wind off Long Island Sound gusted, sending a draft of cold air through a crack in the floorboards. Every time he opened the place, the dankness reminded him of his mother's vegetable keep behind their home in the Pyrenees. Of her vow to take his *cesta,* hide its sickle-shaped jai alai basket until he'd finished storing her onions and garlic deep within the earth. Meanwhile, his friends shouted for him to hurry as they ran along the dusty road, swooping their *cestas,* snatching at *pelotas,* the hand-stitched spheres boys from the next village would hurl at them during the game they were going to play.

Joseba muttered in Spanish, "Lynn's more dangerous than my mother's threat to leave me unarmed." He watched her from behind his computer, where he was checking for loose connections in the USB port for the third time. This is going to be all business, he reminded himself.

Lynn stepped out of her snow-covered boots, hurried across the living room, and lowered a shopping bag onto the coffee table. She reached in and pulled out a magazine. "I brought something to read—in case you get boring." She grinned that maniacal grin of hers, jaws clenched, lips stretched into her cheeks.

"What's with the tropical heat?" Lynn asked, sloughing off her parka. She walked across the room, and wrote her name, one huge letter per windowpane, in the drizzling condensation, then arched her back, and knotted her sandy hair at the base of her neck. The long, elegant neck he'd once tickled with—what had she called them? His "daddy-long-lashes."

"I moved back to Connecticut to get away from the humidity in Miami," she said, her voice whirring along with his computer. He sighed; her unmade-up Saturday face had always been his favorite.

"I couldn't turn the computer on in the cold—besides, I like the heat."

Sweat seeped through the valley between her breasts, darkening her faded maroon jersey. One of his old ones, Joseba wondered? He counted back—it'd been eleven years—and dismissed the thought.

As if this was a practice at the fronton, Joseba pulled his T-shirt out from his trousers, and mopped his eyes, the square of his chin, the dappled gray curls that had recently appeared along the midline of his rock hard belly.

"Years catching up to us, hey, Mr. Txalaparta?" Lynn said, cute and innocent like, pointing to his grays. Holding him in her teasing blue eyes, she waddled to the thermostat. "Mind if I bring it down a notch?"

He turned toward his keyboard, touched the keys with one hand, and shooed at her with the other. "Sure, sure. Lower it." Just like her to take over. Joseba narrowed his eyes, took a drag from his cigarette. Smoke wandered from his nostrils, over his thick moustache. "I stopped smoking ten years ago, and what'd I do first thing after seeing Glenna? Bought a carton of Camels."

This was the first time since the accident Joseba had said her name out loud, and hearing it shocked him. He stared at the cigarette between his thumb and third finger—its smoldering reminded him of the steamy air curling from the steel pipe in Glenna's throat. He reached, his hand shaking, for an ashtray, and stopped, afraid that the act of snuffing might somehow do the same to Glenna.

Sure, he was superstitious, just like all the players on his team. When he and Lynn were still together, she'd teased him about the gold chains mounded around his neck. Tiny horns, god's eyes, rabbits' feet, a miniature *cesta,* and Lynn had rested in his chest hairs. Except the day before a game when ladders, black cats and sex, anything that might sap his strength, terrified him. Glenna's almost dying while driving a car registered in his name had spooked him, made him wonder if her accident had been meant for him.

"Seeing Glenna blew you away, didn't it?"

Joseba dropped his cigarette into the ashtray. Ashes fluttered onto the table, drifted to the floor. He raked his hand through his wavy black hair. "Her eyes follow me. At night, they keep me awake. If I fall asleep, I dream about her in that hospital bed."

"What bothers Glenna most is knowing she'll never be able to do anything for herself." Lynn pointed to his orderly array of equipment. "If you can figure out a way for her to use a computer, you'll be her hero."

"That laminated board those hospital techies gave her really pissed me off." Joseba flicked his lighter at another cigarette, pictured Glenna's communication board, with rectangles numbered one through five and letters in each: A-E in the first, F-J in the next, followed by K-O, P-T and U-Z. A note had been scribbled across a ragged piece of hospital stationery: *Say the number of the section—Glenna will nod when you name the one she wants. Then say the letters in that section—she'll nod when you get to the right one. Repeat until she finishes spelling what she wants to say.*

Joseba paced, the floorboards creaking with every other step. "You'd think those bastards...where's their pride, man?" A guilty shiver prickled his spine. The small incline from the corner of Glenna's cheekbone to the center of her bow-shaped upper lip had wilted into a corpse's pose. And the force that once pulsed throughout her body was gone —except for the look in her honey-green eyes that pleaded with him in his dreams, "Don't forget, Joseba, I'm in here."

Joseba blinked. "So, how long have you been working at the hospital?"

"Six weeks."

"When I walked into Glenna's room, I wasn't sure it was you, until you started talking." Joseba looked Lynn over, rested a beat too long on her heart-shaped hips, and soft bulging belly. Her eyes caught him staring. "You've changed," he said.

"Ninety pounds worth," Lynn said, folding her hands across her chest.

"You had that killer instinct, that pounding drive to win at volleyball—at everything you did. I never guessed you would…"

Lynn arched her narrow eyebrow, "Plump out?" Her hands slid over her hips, down the curve of her buttocks.

"No, become a nurse."

"At twenty-three, I started resenting the pre-dawn work-outs, the trainers telling me when and what to eat, where to go, and what time to be home. Once my team won the gold, I got bored with hanging around airports, checking in and out of hotels. The morning I called the front desk to find out which country I was in, I knew I was in trouble." Lynn took a chocolate *Kiss* out of her pocket, and grinned. "I'm surprised you're still a jock."

Joseba sat by the bay window. Waves slithered from shore then rumbled in, vomiting scummy foam over the sand. She was lying; she had to be. Winning meant too much to her. Before the games in Barcelona, Lynn spent hours watching videos of her opponents, memorizing their moves—good and bad—and planning how to use them to her advantage. After her team won the Olympics, offers of endorsements were scattered along their kitchen counter like ticker tape after a New York parade—she was riding higher than he'd ever been—until he married her younger sister. From then on, he'd stayed the hell away from her, didn't want her studying his moves.

"When Phoebe told me you'd gone to nursing school, I pictured you, the adrenaline junkie, in the ER with overdoses, heart attacks, and stab victims." He flashed his boyish dimples hoping she'd forgiven him for being a shit.

"I was in the ER the night Glenna was admitted. Fire department had to pry her out of her sports car."

The sudden movement of Joseba's chair against the wide plank floors echoed. He stood up and walked across the room. "A Sprite—*che* was driving a Sprite," Joseba muttered, confusing 'ch' for 'sh' a nervous habit of his.

"What?"

"Glenna sold antique sports cars. *Che* was bringing an Austin Healy Sprite to my office, for me to test drive. I'd been looking for one for Phoebe, for her birthday," he lied.

Lynn frowned, but didn't seem surprised. Joseba's eyes got filmy. "Damn it." He slapped his wide, thick hand on the table, almost toppled the computer tower.

"How long had you been shopping?" Lynn asked.

Joseba sensed her sniffing around, knew he should sidestep her question, but couldn't bring himself to care. "Almost two years."

"Sweet of you to do that for my sister. You know how much Phoebe loves sexy cars. Next time, I hope you'll find another way to show your undying devotion." Lynn's voice was as bald as the newscaster on *Alive at Six*.

Joseba checked her expression to see if she was being sarcastic, but couldn't tell; she'd popped the *Kiss* in her mouth, and was busy peeling the foil from another. He pictured Glenna in his Sprite, her Jackie O sunglasses covering her petite features, an Italian silk scarf trailing her, one gloved hand downshifting, and the other guiding the wheel along the curving roadway. He slid down in his chair; the scent of chocolate made him want to gag.

"She's twenty-two," Joseba said, his voice a whimper.

"Who are you kidding? Phoebe's going on thirty-four."

"No, Glenna. I'm talking about Glenna." Joseba picked up the scallop shell Phoebe had found last summer, closed it in his palm, and squeezed until it splintered.

"I thought she was kind of young to afford the gorgeous pink cashmere number she was wearing."

"What are you talking about?"

Lynn narrowed her eyes. "I had to undress her, fast, so I used a scissors. Later, when I dumped her outfit in the biohazard pail, I found the label, *Tailored especially for Glenna Paterson*."

Joseba knew the suit. He'd had it made so upscale clients would turn her way the second they walked into the showroom. He shook his head, guessed that the antique diamond, and emerald pin she'd had on her lapel was now a biohazard, too.

"Do me a favor?" Joseba reached out to Lynn. "Toss this for me?"

She moved closer. "No problem." He emptied the jagged shells into her palm. "I'll make some coffee, too."

Such a generous offer—too generous. Joseba knew her crazy smile and twinkling blue eyes meant she'd already worked out a stunt to remind him she wasn't his maid. *They were so much alike*, Joseba thought, *it's no wonder they didn't make it together*. The lid on the trash can in the kitchen snapped up, and Lynn clapped her hands a few times. Then the lid crashed, just like their life together.

After Lynn had figured out he'd been financing his Rolls Royce, and their exotic vacations with payoffs for throwing a game or two, she went righteous on him, insisted he return the money. He refused, and thought she'd forgotten about it until the night she listened to a message one of the fronton groupies had left on his answering machine. Then she remembered that and every other sin he'd committed. She locked him out of his ocean front condo, hollered, "Go back where you came from!" and tossed his keys off the veranda into the muck of low tide.

The aroma of the decaf coffee Phoebe always bought seeped into the room. No matter how many times Joseba had told her the smell reminded him of the ghetto in New Haven, where his mother and father had lived after leaving Basque, she still bought it, out of spite, he was sure. He couldn't blame her. While neither of them had ever said it aloud, they both knew his marrying her had something to do with Lynn.

At first, Joseba felt badly about using Phoebe until he talked to his friend, Ramon. Ramon had said he was a fool to worry. "Phoebe's been dating jai alai players for years. She's seen other babes swap jocks—even when they're ugly, like you." Joseba laughed. Ever since they'd been kids, Ramon had called him ugly, even though Ramon was the one with the scar.

Joseba smiled a sad smile. He'd landed his *cesta* on Ramon's forehead after Ramon admitted to keeping secrets. To not telling Joseba his mother had contacted Dr. Whitcomb, the local hack.

"Here's the reason he's always getting into fights," his mother had said, pressing Joseba's head toward the window so Dr. Whitcomb could see the unusually short skin anchoring his tongue to the bottom of his mouth. "No wonder he can't talk right," she said.

The doctor had peered through his dusty glasses and nodded, then turned toward the sink, and washed his hands. He dried them on the towel and, as if he were a hungry fisherman with a huge clamshell, pried open his black bag. "Close your eyes and open your mouth," he said. And jerk that he was, Joseba did what he was told. The doctor snipped, blood spurted, and Joseba screamed like hell.

Lynn backed through the swinging door, balancing a tray with two steaming mugs.

"This is the first time this week I've run this program. I was waiting for you to help me adjust it to Glenna's..."

"Condition?" she asked, and handed him his coffee.

He took it, and glanced sideways at Lynn who was running her fingertips over the chipped edges of a snail's shell by his computer. "When Phoebe and I were kids, we spent hours searching for perfect shells." Lynn wandered to the thermostat and turned down the heat.

"I can't concentrate when I'm cold." Joseba crossed the room, and flicked at the small dial. The furnace groaned.

Lynn tossed the shell in the air, caught it, tossed it again. "When I got tired of that game, I told Phoebe there are no perfect shells."

Joseba set his coffee down at the far end of the table. "Then what'd she do?"

"Married you."

"*Oush.*" Joseba clutched his fist to his heart in mock pain. Lynn's smirking made him wish he'd used a word that didn't give his nerves away.

"So, tell me again. How am I supposed to help with this project?" She drifted behind him, stared at the monitor.

"When Phoebe gets here, I want you to talk her into easing up on her ad campaign."

"I thought I was here to help you write Glenna's program."

"That too. You spend a lot of time with Glenna. Tell me the kinds of things she wants to talk about, that way I can put them into the computer." Configurations of symbols and numbers rolled from top to bottom along the monitor. Joseba highlighted some and clicked on others. "This isn't working the way I thought it would. At this rate, it's gonna take months."

Lynn sat on the sofa, picked up her magazine, and flipped the pages.

Joseba leaned back in the chair, gave his continental cut trousers a tug, then rested his ankle on his knee to form the thick triangle where he set his keyboard. He clacked away, his Italian knit shirt pushed up to his elbows. Blue veins bulged beneath his hairy forearms, powerful wrists, and buffed nails.

A small gray window appeared on the monitor, asking him if he wanted the computer to remember his email password. Joseba positioned his mouse on NO—hell no.

He watched Lynn get up, and move about the living room, sipping coffee, checking the clock, probably wondering when Phoebe was going to show up, while he emailed his buddy, Ramon, in Miami:

- Good to hear from you, man. Timing couldn't be better. I'm in deep shit. My old lady's sister's here, pacing and talking—god, her voice still gets to me, deep and husky like Lauren Bacall's. Remember Lynn, from Spain? Played volleyball in the '92 Olympics in

Barcelona? Thighs like a guy's, arms long and lean, and an ass so tight you used to say, "She ought to carry a weapon permit for that thing." Don't get too excited—she's gained ninety pounds.

Within seconds, Ramon wrote back:

- You sound bummed, man. What's going on? Wife giving you a rough time?

- Hell no. Well, sort of. Phoebe's Madison Avenue agency is hot to unleash an advertising blitz for the program I told you about, Computer Think. She wears buttons that say *Share Your Thoughts* and *Think, Don't Touch* that kind of thing. She even contacted some Association for the Brain Injured, and offered my services, giving demos at their international conference, with the media there, of course. Trouble is, the program's not finished. I need to get the bugs worked out. The whole thing's getting on my nerves...

- Why? You're gonna make millions (not that you need it).

- I told you about that woman in the car accident.

- You doing what I think you were doing, old man?

- Yeah, and it's eating away at me. I'm
  sorry about what's done, and sorrier for
  her future.
- What's that supposed to mean?

Joseba's hands went limp. He took a couple of deep breaths, put his fingers back on the keyboard and typed:

- Now that she really needs me, I'm afraid
  I'm not good enough to help her. I've
  hired consultants, but there's still a lot I
  don't know. If it were the other way
  around, she'd figure out how to help me.
  She's the smartest woman I ever met. I
  never had to say a word to her; she
  always knew how to make me feel like a
  better man than I ever was.

"Something the matter, Joseba? You're looking kind of pale," Lynn said, lifting his *cesta* from its rack above the fireplace. Brittle, it creaked as she shifted it around, and blew off the dust. "Remember when you broke the world's record for speed?"

Joseba nodded. "You attached a brass plaque inscribed with *ONE HUNDRED AND THIRTY MILES PER HOUR* to the *cesta* I used during that game. That night, you climbed on the bar, and hung it from the ceiling at The Fronton Follies. You were wearing really tight pants. The guys cheered and whistled." He checked out the skin dimpled against the seat of her purple sweat pants, and sighed. "I guess neither of us is any good at losing."

Lynn set his *cesta* on the mantle. "You're right."

Joseba clacked on the keyboard, louder and harder than usual, then stood up and reached for an oversized eyeglass case. "Let me show you what I've done with this program so far." He slipped on a pair of frames with compass-like dials, flashing sensors, and wires connected to electrodes. "The final product won't be this crude. When the electrodes are held in place with a suction cup, Glenna will be able to work the computer by thinking the commands instead of using the keyboard or the mouse." Joseba was talking fast.

Lynn came closer. "Those are the weirdest looking…"

The door opened, and a burst of chill wind whisked Joseba's papers from the table, driving them against the wall before they collapsed to the floor.

"Oh my gawd, Joseba, the frames are fantastic—real science fictiony. Stay there, let me get that shot for the promo materials." Phoebe pushed her oversized glasses onto her head, raked her wavy auburn hair away from her square face. "Where's my camera when I need it?" She searched through her black leather handbag, clicking her tongue and muttering, "Oh damn, that's not it. Here we go."

"Now look at the monitor like you're telling it what to do—that's good, don't move." Phoebe pressed the button on her digital camera. The strobe flashed, the flash went off, and Phoebe smiled. "Nothing like showing up and going right to work," she said, giving her sister a peck on the cheek, and blowing a kiss at Joseba.

"I had the most fantastic morning. First we got the web site up and running— www.Glenna.com—isn't that the best? Then we put the finishing touches on Glenna's story, a human interest kind of thing. We're sending it to Stone Phillips—he agreed to run Glenna as a feature story. He's going to interview her in her hospital room, and he wants to interview you, too, Joseba. I'll tell you the exact date as soon as I find my Palm Pilot. Wait a sec, here it is..." Phoebe unwrapped her six-foot scarf, shrugged off her jacket, and reached into her handbag. "This time I don't have to dig," she said, straightening her cashmere sweater over her slim hips.

Pink. The color hit Joseba first. The same shade he'd bought for Glenna. Same neckline, same ribbed style. His shoulders slumped, and he skulked down into his chair. He took the glasses off, rested his head on his wrist. Phoebe waved her Palm Pilot at him. He looked away; she was making him dizzy.

"Joseba, remember the first day you saw Glenna after her accident, and how upset you were about that communication board? Well, I didn't tell you, but I wrote down everything you said, and we've included it in the packet we're sending the network. You were brilliant—want to hear it?" Phoebe opened a folder with 'GLENNA' written across the top, and slipped her glasses down onto her nose.

Joseba stared. Phoebe owned at least twenty pairs of reading glasses, different colors and styles to go with whatever she was wearing. "A fashion accessory," she called them, like earrings or scarves. Against her lawyer's advice, she wrote them off as a business expense, called them a "must have" in the advertising industry, like her artsy conference room or glitzy car. "The first fifteen seconds a client lays eyes on me makes or breaks a deal," she'd said.

"New glasses?" Joseba asked.

Phoebe smiled. "I told Lynn about a client of mine who's writing a book about Jackie Kennedy, and Lynn bought them for me as an early birthday present, along with this sweater. You like?"

Joseba steadied himself on the table, and thought he was going to be sick.

Lynn laughed that deep throaty laugh of hers. "There's a funky retro shop in the Village that specializes in Jackie O memorabilia...pink pillbox hats with matching boucle suits, scarves, and those glasses. I had to get them for Phoebe." Lynn looked at Joseba, wrinkled her nose. "It's a sister thing."

Phoebe stood up and looked in the mirror. "I brought them to my optometrist, and he fitted them with new lenses. Everyone loves them. Now, before I forget, listen to this excerpt from the piece I wrote about you:

Cardboard, colored letters, the alphabet—chunked into groups of five—these were the tools of his boyhood.

Years later, in Glenna's hospital room, Joseba hoped the laminated communication board he'd found there was nothing more than a misplaced art project, like the ones he'd made when he was in grade school. He could almost smell the spicy white paste his teacher had kept on the shelf, beneath her faded green alphabet cards. He recalled sliding his fingers down the side of the jar, scooping paste in to his mouth, it melting down his throat. "Hmm, good." The girls beside him squealed, "That's gross." And that's how Joseba described the lack of technology for someone in Glenna's condition. "Gross."

"Is that amazing, or what?" Phoebe asked, sinking into her sister's hug.

Joseba unfolded a paper clip, and twisted it until it snapped in two. "Great, it's great."

"Time for the champagne I brought for Phoebe's birthday," Lynn said, pulling an insulated box from her shopping bag.

Phoebe peeked into the bag. "Fantastic. My sister brought champagne glasses, too. Oh Joseba, you're not going to fool around with that now, are you?"

Stooped over his keyboard, Joseba finished his email to Ramon... *this feels like the top player just walloped one off the side wall, and I'm too close to return the shot...*and closed his email.

Joseba heard a popping sound and looked up.

"For you." Lynn handed him a plastic glass filled with champagne. Its bubbles churned to the surface, and exploded.

"A toast. To my sister, the advertising wizardess." Lynn sounded like one of the announcers at the fronton: loud, important, bursting with the latest score.

Phoebe and Lynn tapped their glasses together, raised them towards Joseba, grinned, and waited for him to return their salute. He edged out from behind the table, glass in hand. Champagne sloshed, forming miniature waves that threatened to break over the side.

Phoebe waited, her pink arm extended, the winter white of her small wrist showing from beneath the cashmere. Joseba thought of Glenna as he touched his glass to Phoebe's.

"Wait, I forgot something," Lynn said, and set her glass on the coffee table. She poked one arm into her shopping bag, and pulled out a small package. Wrapped in gold rice paper, it reminded Joseba of the paper he and Lynn had bought many years back, when they were vacationing in Japan, and of the shopkeeper who explained how coarse threads became smooth paper only after being pressed between two huge rollers.

Lynn winked at Joseba, and set the package in the palm of his hand.

Although it weighed an ounce, maybe two, instinct told Joseba not to underestimate its power. "For me?" he asked, with a confused half-cocked smile.

Lynn rolled her eyes, sighed in mock exasperation, and sidled up to him. She cupped her hand to his ear, and in her loudest whisper said, "You forgot, silly. You bought it, and asked me to wrap it for your wife's birthday." She stepped back, and gestured for him to give Phoebe her gift.

Phoebe raised her shoulders, brought her hands to her lips, and looked back and forth between Joseba and Lynn. Lynn beamed at Joseba. Joseba froze.

After Glenna's accident, mourning and guilt had overtaken him, throwing him off balance, destroying the routines Phoebe had come to expect. So far, he hadn't gotten around to buying a gift for Phoebe, and he sure as hell hadn't given it to Lynn to wrap.

Joseba felt Lynn tapping his elbow. "Go ahead—Phoebe's waiting."

Like the young boy whose friends had urged him to join the game, he handed the gift to Phoebe.

"We usually go to a fancy, New York restaurant for dinner on my birthday so this is…" She motioned to the living room with its worn furnishings. "…funky."

Phoebe dropped the torn rice paper into Joseba's hand, and opened a small rosewood jeweler's box. From a velvet cushion, she lifted an antique diamond and emerald pin. It sparkled in the cold December light. "Oh, Joseba," she said, throwing her arms around his neck. "It's perfect." Joseba felt his lips make contact with her slippery pink lip-gloss. She pressed the empty rosewood box into his palm, and positioned the pin on her sweater.

"Here or here?" she was saying to Lynn as she moved the pin from her left shoulder to her right.

Joseba looked at the pin against Phoebe's sweater, saw it as sharp and shinny, and recalled the arch of blood spurting from his mouth, hitting the sink, and splattering to the floor. He'd clamped his mouth shut, and, seconds later, when it filled with blood, spit it out, never saying a word, refusing to give his mother the satisfaction of knowing how much it hurt. Lynn had caught him by surprise and landed a *remate*, a killer shot. She'd set him up so well, he'd never seen it coming. Now, they were even. In a way, he was glad.

WINE GUY

Within seconds of settling herself on the barstool that stormy evening, my friend Marty had the new owner, a cocky guy wearing a starched chef's hat, ready to sign on for thralldom. Marty's snow-covered blond hair framed her plain, yet vibrant features: teasing green eyes, a quick smile, girlish blush, plus a birth date that landed this side of middle age. "I want a glass of red wine, but I can't decide which." Her voice commanded that giddy, flirtatious quality I'd somehow lost.

"Here, I'll let you taste a couple," the guy said, whipping two huge goblets from the overhead rack. "I'll start you off with a red Zin from California and an Australian Shiraz." He filled each glass more than half, gave one, then the other a swirl, then slid them towards Marty.

"I love wine-tasting parties," she purred.

I sipped from the glass of ice water the guy's wife had given me while I'd been waiting for Marty to arrive for our long-awaited get-together. Now, the pine bar's soft polyurethane gloss reflected Marty's graceful hands traveling from her cheeks to the goblets to her wet bangs. She cooed over each glass of wine, sniffed, swirled, and claimed she didn't know which to sample first.

"We have a great wine collection," the guy said, pointing to the bottles on the mirrored shelf behind him, where an assortment of labels glittered beneath the seductive lighting.

"You must know a lot about wine," Marty said, sipping the Zinfandel. I admired her style—the ease with which she honed in on this man's sensibilities.

The guy leaned on the bar, his medieval headgear grazing the crown of Marty's head with an intimate nonchalance. "Tell you my secret—I've got a fantastic salesman. He's the brains who keeps me stocked." I lowered my eyes in embarrassment.

"Do you have any Sangiovese?" I asked, recalling the bottle of wine my husband, Carl, ordered during our recent trip to Tuscany when he raised his glass in the shimmering candlelight and toasted me. "To my Sarah, many happy years of retirement. After thirty years at the university, you've earned it."

"See the legs on that baby? That means it's a great wine," the guy said to Marty, who was holding the Zinfandel to the light, admiring its purple-mahogany hue.

"It's so pretty, I wish I could find a dress this color." She sipped, swished appreciatively, then swallowed. "Um, peppery, with a hint of cinnamon." The guy shifted from his left to his right elbow, and torqued his starched white back towards me.

The tiny lines around my lips pursed into worried crevasses. Wait staff shouldering platters shot him disgusted looks as they hustled from the kitchen to the adjoining dining room. More patrons entered, stomped snow from their boots, and seeing the length of the queue, donned aggrieved expressions.

I repositioned the small gift bag I'd brought for Marty on the stool beside me, munched on a salty Goldfish cracker, and estimated how long this wine guy, no doubt, a first-time owner, would remain in business. I'd seen kids like him in my English classes: almost good-looking, and not smart-enough for college, who'd managed to fool an admission's officer into thinking their Hollywood-hip images had Nobel Laureate potential. They never made it past the first semester. I gave him a generous six months.

Marty, meanwhile, swished Shiraz around her sensitive palate, swallowed, then commented on the subtlety of the black currant. Impressed, I drew stick figures in the moisture coating my glass. "They're both so good, I still can't decide," she whimpered, and the guy brought out a couple more bottles for her to try.

"I know what *I'd* like," I said. Marty's new friend glanced at me, or rather, through me. That wouldn't have happened if my hair were still waist length, raven black, and my figure slight. I crossed and uncrossed my legs in amused boredom.

"Shiraz is one of my favorites. I'll have a glass of that." I marveled at my need to justify my choice of beverages; service seemed to depend on winning this bozo's approval.

"I'm going to have the Zinfandel," Marty announced, after a final taste test.

"Thank goodness," I murmured. The proud barkeep replenished Marty's tasting glass. I repeated my order. The guy pried his gaze from Marty, and turned to me.

My back had started to ache. I squirmed on the barstool and decided I wasn't going to repeat my selection. The wine guy raised his arm, fingers poised to remove a glass from the overhead rack, then stopped.

He turned, eyed Marty's half-full glass of Shiraz, then slid her lipstick-stained goblet toward me. "Here, you can have this."

I hoped Marty wouldn't glance at the mirror, where my horrified expression starred back. I slipped my arms into my coat, and picked up my handbag. "Catch you later," I said, pecked Marty's cheek, and murmured something about having to meet Carl.

"Going already? Be careful driving in the snow," she said.

"How was everything?" the wine guy's wife asked from behind the hostess' podium.

"Three months," I said. "I give your wine-guy three months." I pressed my shoulder to the door, car keys griped in one hand, the other hanging heavy at my side. As much as I wished I could laugh at the humor of the situation, I couldn't. I tightened my fist around what felt like an untidy package of leftovers: my doggie bag of humiliation.

WHISPER NOTES

The last time Ian had seen his daughter she was hurrying down the aisle during her mother's funeral, the staccato of her heels echoing against the marble floor, her cell phone plastered to her ear. Now, Ariana sat behind the wheel of her rusty white Suburban, smoking a cigarette, and waiting. Ian quickened his pace, cut through his neighbors' yards, past the azaleas, rhododendron, and weeping yews that bordered his unit at the Portland Harbor View Condominiums. He hurried across his front lawn, arms tensed, ready to wrap her in the octopus hug she once loved when she rolled down the window. "For God's sake, Daddy, we've been waiting for almost an hour. Where you been?"

"I got back from the store, and decided to go for a walk," he said, frowning.

"What's the matter?"

He tapped his watch and brought it to his ear. "I had it all planned. I was going to make linguine and clam sauce to celebrate your first night home, but now I can't—the fish market just closed." His thin shoulders slumped. Ariana hopped out of her van, and walked toward him, shaking her head.

He reached for her, but when he caught sight of her fringed pink blouse clinging like Saran wrap to her lacey bra, he plunged his hands into his pockets and pecked her cheek.

Ariana looped her arm in his, and led him to her van. She pointed to the digital alarm clock on her dashboard. *Friday, 5:15* glowed in neon green. "How about I get you one of those, for your house-warming gift?"

Ian sat in the driver's seat to get a better look. Lipstick-stained cigarette butts overflowed the ashtray, and stale smoke combined with the pine scent of a flat dangling Christmas tree cutout. He held his breath, and picked up a couple of Dunkin' Donuts' coffee cups. "How about a box of trash bags for your homecoming present?" He checked to make sure she was still smiling, then smiled back. "Never mind dinner, I just want to meet my grandson—where is the little man?" A muffled screech came from beneath a blanket in the back seat.

"What in the world?" Ian put his hand on the tattered upholstery and twisted himself around.

"Daddy, this is Gabriel," Ariana said, and hoisted herself onto the back seat. A tow-headed boy popped up, touched his forehead to Ian's knuckles, and shook his hands as if covered by angry bees. Thick glasses curtained his cheekbones, making his speckled blue eyes look bigger than normal.

"What's he doing?" The boy stopped flailing, and turned his ear toward Ian.

Ariana frowned. "He doesn't like it when anyone rearranges his stuff."

"You mean the coffee cups?"

Ariana nodded. "He was playing with them."

Gabriel threw himself against his seat, bounced forward and back. Ian pulled away, bumped his spine against the dashboard, his head on the rear-view mirror.

Ariana slipped a grimy flannel blanket around Gabriel's shoulders, and wrapped him, papoose-like. Ian gaped. Ariana glanced up. "Don't worry, he likes this."

Ian got out of the van, peered at the cocooned figure through the smudged rear window. Suddenly exhausted, he leaned his head against the warm car.

"Daddy, are you okay?"

He stared at the macadam where his neighbor's grandchildren played hopscotch, and never wailed when the sprinkler washed away their chalky grids. "It's the heat," Ian said, peeling off his sports coat, and folding it over his arm. Ariana looked at him, her mother's golden curls tumbling like bunched grapes along her forehead. Thread-like lines splayed across her cheeks toward the edge of her oval face. Her eyes seemed deeper than he'd remembered.

"I didn't mean to sound so…" Ian opened his arms, but she scurried off. "I should have checked to see when you were going to get here—now, we'll have to order pizza for dinner," he said, following her to the back of her van.

"That's okay. There are a few things I should have checked with you, too." She tugged at the tailgate until it opened, lifted a box, and dropped it in his arms. Ian swayed, until Ariana grabbed his elbow. "Didn't mean to throw you off balance."

She helped Ian carry the box up the brick walk, and gawked when he opened the door. "Amazing," she said. A grand piano gleamed in the filtered sunlight.

Situated by a bank of floor-to-ceiling windows, his lone trophy rested in the middle of his empty showcase. "This is my favorite room," Ian said, as they lowered the box to the floor.

Ariana wandered in, her footsteps echoing. "A Steinway," she murmured, and approached the piano tourist-like, gliding her fingertips over the urns and garlands embedded in its cinnamon burl veneer. "This must have cost a fortune. What happened to the rest of your furniture?"

Ian had bought the piano as a reward for the years he'd spent managing her mother's career in the opera. Elegant and expensive like Leonora, it spanned six foot ten inches and cost seventy thousand dollars. At first, he wasn't going to buy it until he read that the New York studio where it'd been restored was located two blocks from one of the world's most prestigious concert venues. Then he had to have it. After all, it was the closest any piano he played would get to Carnegie Hall.

"This is a genuine 1924 Victorian Artcase—I thought it deserved a place of its own," Ian said. Ariana scowled as she eyed his minimalist décor. "Come on, I'll help you unload your suitcases," he said, and motioned her outside.

They lugged box after box, suitcase after gym bag into the house, piling them against the wall in the guestroom beneath the family collection of degrees from the New England Conservatory of Music. To the left, his BA, magna cum laude, with Leonora's to the right, and Ariana's, dated May 8, 1993, in the middle. Beside them, his wife's most prestigious plaques: the McAllister Award, the Elena Obraztsova International Competition, and the ARIA. By itself, to the far right, a fading black and white photo of him at the piano with Ariana on his lap, starting the lessons he'd hoped would inspire her to outdistance the family legacy.

Ariana wedged the toe of her cowboy boot in the door, waited for Ian to pass, then let it slam behind her. "Aren't you going to wake Gabriel?" he asked. She stacked another box on the growing pile, unaware she'd blocked her mother's name from his view.

"Nothing bothers him when he's napping." Ariana peered at Ian. "You look like you could use a rest, too. Have a seat, I'll finish this."

Ian edged through the rows of boxes, stepped over laundry baskets loaded with miniature jeans and jockey shorts, and slumped into the wicker chair in the corner. Ariana's writing looped across the side of each box: "Bedroom." "Bathroom." "Kitchen." "Personal." "Music." "Gabriel." He lifted the last box. It was light, weighted in the middle. He turned it over, picked at the masking tape until its edges curled, and put it down.

He looked around. Sometime in the last hour, Ariana had moved the furniture Ian had saved—her childhood canopy bed and hand-painted bureau where she once stored her treasures—and jammed them against the window. She'd shoved her mother's rosewood music stand into the closet, and covered the cot where Gabriel would sleep with bags of stuffed animals. When she returned he asked, "Didn't you say this was going to be a quick visit?"

"Don't worry, it's not as bad as it looks," Ariana said. Her face melted into the pout she'd used on him when she was a kid. "Texas finally got to me. I'm going to find a place here in Portland. I have an appointment with a Realtor, and I've lined up an audition for a gig." She jerked her head toward the electric keyboard cradled in her arms.

"I thought the dampness aggravated your allergies."

"Charlie aggravated my allergies. I left him in Kerville. My lawyer's drawing up the papers."

"And that welt on the back of your thigh? Did Charlie aggravate that, too?" Ian's voice became louder. He sank his nails into his palms.

"Gabriel hit me with his baseball bat, by accident."

Her mother used to say the eyes tell all, but Ariana's told him so little. He took the keyboard from her, wrapped his fingers around its lifeless keys. It was what he hated about electric pianos. Until they're plugged in, they have no voice.

"Ohhh nooo." A wail came from the van.

"That's Gabriel," Ariana said, rushing into the foyer, and out the door.

She returned, clutching Gabriel with one hand, and a Walmart bag in the other. "This is Granddaddy's house. Mommy and Gabriel are going to stay in Granddaddy's house until Mommy finds a new place for Mommy and Gabriel to live."

They went into the bathroom, and closed the door. Ian listened to Ariana saying, "Nice job," and "No splashing." Gabriel opened the door, headed to the dining room table, and climbed on a chair. "Gabriel needs to stay there while Mommy makes Gabriel's dinner." Ariana rummaged in the bag, pulled out a magic wand, and handed it to him.

"Isn't he too old for you to be talking to him like that?" Ian asked.

"He has trouble with language, and pronouns really mess him up." She walked into the kitchen.

Gabriel tipped the wand first to the left, then the right, spellbound by tiny glittering stars, half moons and hearts tumbling in slow motion through an oily liquid. Such intense focus, almost moronic, if not for the flexibility of his tapered fingers, smooth knuckles, and tendons gliding along the backs of his intelligent hands. Ian looked at his own hands, then at the boy's; except for their size and childhood vitality, Gabriel's mirrored his.

Ariana planted her hands on her hips. "Daddy?" Her impatient voice, almost a whine. "It's time for Gabriel's dinner."

Ian looked up. "I'll order a pizza."

"Gabriel won't eat anything that takes a lot of chewing. I brought his dinner." Ariana pulled a blue box of macaroni and cheese from the Walmart bag and, set it on the counter. "How about putting water on for pasta?"

Ian filled a small pan with water while Ariana tied a Sesame Street bib around Gabriel's neck. Mesmerized by his magic wand, he ignored his mother.

"Does he always do that?" Ian asked as he positioned the pan on the stove, and turned on the burner.

"Any chance he gets. The doctor calls it 'self-stimulation.' Says it's part of being autistic."

"Autistic?" Ian's bristly silver eyebrows collapsed into a line across his forehead.

Ariana drained the pasta, and stirred in the packet of yellow powder until it turned thick and gooey. When she placed his food in front of him, Gabriel separated the macaroni into three small mounds and, working counterclockwise, shoveled one elbow pasta at a time into his mouth until his cheeks puffed like a chipmunk's. Then he swallowed.

Ian squinted in disgust. "He's got some strange eating habits. Is that because he's…autistic?" The word caught in his throat.

"He just started feeding himself six months ago."

"You've had to feed him all this time?"

Ariana nodded. "Why do you think I never came home when Mom was so sick?"

"Your mother and I knew something was wrong, but we never guessed it was Gabriel. All we had were the pictures you sent, and they made him look so...normal."

"Gabriel wouldn't even let Charlie feed him. I took a big chance coming home when Mom died."

"Was Charlie the one who called during your mother's funeral?" Ariana took a deep breath, and nodded. "Why didn't you tell me about Gabriel?" Ian asked softly. Gabriel's spoon clicked against his plate.

"I did. I told you one night, a long time ago, when we were on the phone, 'Gabriel's autistic.' I didn't think you needed the details. You had enough to deal with, what with Mom's chemo and all. Besides..." She pulled a crushed pack of Marlboro's out of her pocket. "I remember trying to meet your standards when I was a kid. I couldn't. And Charlie sure as hell didn't. If you think for a second I was going to put Gabriel through that..."

"Autistic? You said autistic?" Ian looked out the kitchen window at his weeping yews. "I thought you said artistic." Autistic—artistic. The words tumbled in his head. He pictured the small yellow van that stopped across the street to pick up the kids who didn't fit on the regular school bus: the droolers, flailers, the ones whose mothers stayed with them, even though they were in their teens. Ian wasn't sure what troubled him more: having a damaged grandson or embarrassing himself in front of his daughter. *His hearing was pitch perfect—how could he have confused these words,* he asked himself? He blushed; he knew the answer.

"Ohhh nooo," Gabriel cooed.

"Gabriel ate all the macaroni. Good job. Time for Mommy to give Gabriel a bath." Ariana untied his bib, and lifted him from the chair. Clutching his magic wand, he wrapped his arms and legs around her as if he were a chimpanzee.

"I'll fill the tub for you."

"Don't bother, he won't sit in the water. He likes to stand while I give him a sponge bath."

"Then I'll order a pizza. It should be here by the time you're done."

"Get a small one for yourself, Daddy. I'm not hungry."

"What about a beer? I bought Heineken, your favorite."

"Now, you're talking."

"Glad to do something right," Ian mumbled as he grabbed two beers with one hand, and lifted a couple of frosty mugs from the freezer with the other. He lowered them to the counter where they clinked with a double thud that reminded him of their evening ritual in the days Leonora was well, shortly after she'd finished her last European tour, and before they'd learned of her brain tumor. He couldn't decide which made him more proud: sitting in the audience during one of her flawless opening nights, or holding her fragile hand while she performed her final act with such courage and dignity. Yes, he'd confused what Ariana had told him—and he was glad.

Leonora had gone to her grave believing their grandson was like her. Artistic.

He made a couple of cheese sandwiches, one for him and the other for Ariana, in case she changed her mind, put them and the mugs on a tray, and crossed the dining room. With the tray balanced between his arm and chest, he opened the patio door. "I'll be outside," he called. He set the tray on the patio table, and dragged an Adirondack chair across the cement, closer to the door where he could hear if Ariana needed him. He positioned the other chair within a hand's reach. Then he sipped his beer and waited.

"Gabriel is going to play while Mommy talks with Granddaddy," Ariana said as she ushered him out of the guestroom. Dressed in solid blue pajama bottoms and a Spider-Man top, his wet hair withdrawing into curls, Gabriel trailed his mother through the living room, stopping at his place at the dining room table. "Granddaddy cleaned up for Mommy. Gabriel will have to wait until tomorrow for more macaroni and cheese." She picked up her cigarettes, and slid the door open until Gabriel followed her outside. He walked to Ian's rose garden as if he'd been there before, and stood with his face toward the wind.

"Your mother used to say, 'the evening breeze scatters remnants of the day, and makes room for tomorrow.'"

Ariana lit a cigarette, inhaled deeply, and let the smoke drift out her nostrils. She sipped her beer, and leaned back in the chair. "Do you know what Gabriel's favorite bedtime story is?"

Ian shook his head. "Rumpelstiltskin. Isn't that weird? That's what Mom used to read to me."

The first time Leonora had read it to Ariana, Ariana cried bitterly when she realized Rumplestiltskin had been promised one thing and given another. "It's not fair," she had repeated until she'd fallen asleep.

Ariana ground her cigarette on the cement, leaving a small dark circle. She dropped the squashed filter in her palm, and swatted at the mosquitoes. "Time for Gabriel's bedtime story. Say goodnight to Granddaddy." She got up and opened the door. Gabriel smiled at the wind, and walked past Ian into the condo. Ariana stopped. "I'm gonna turn in early, too."

Ian watched her disappear around the corner. He sipped his beer, and stared at the crimson glow ribboning the horizon. "You were right, Ariana. Tricking that old gnome wasn't fair."

Awoken in the middle of the night by an unsettling cacophony of whistles and bird-like twittering, Ian tiptoed down the hall, peeked in the guestroom. Ariana snored softly while, in the dim shadow of the nightlight, Gabriel fluttered his fingers inches from his eyes, and recited that afternoon's conversation verbatim, capturing every inflection from curiosity to anger to disbelief: "Why didn't you tell me about Gabriel? I did. I told you one night, a long time ago, when we were on the phone, 'Gabriel's autistic.' I didn't think you needed the details. You had enough to deal with, what with Mom's chemo and all."

Ian shook his head. Was he dreaming? He held his breath, clutched the doorjamb, and leaned into the room. Was that his grandson? Did Ariana know? He scanned the boxes for a tape recorder, and, finding none, squinted at Gabriel who kept on talking: "Besides...I remember trying to meet your standards when I was a kid. I couldn't. And Charlie sure as hell didn't. If you think for a second I was going to put Gabriel through that...Autistic? You said autistic? I thought you said artistic." Ian gasped, an audible sound, and Gabriel fell silent as if nothing had happened.

The next morning, coffee mug in hand, Ian leaned wearily against the piano. He gazed at the Ferguson family tree hanging on the dining room wall, then at his grandson. Seated on a pillow that boosted his bony chest and arms to table height, the diapered king dangled a julienne strip of mango, jellyrolled his tongue, and sucked it into his mouth. Ariana hovered over the kitchen island humming *Your Cheating Heart,* and sliced the second half of Gabriel's butterscotch-colored breakfast. "I'll join you in a minute," she said. "I have to feed him first. If he doesn't get exactly the same food, at the same time, he'll have a tantrum you'll never forget."

"Like someone else I know," whispered Ian. Despite her childhood tendency to be ill-tempered in the morning, he found little similarity between the boy and his mother. Ariana's features always mirrored whatever was going on inside her. Ian studied his grandson. He'd inherited his mother's beauty, but not a wrinkle of her expressiveness.

Ian sighed. Even his old golden lab had had expressions. He would thump his thick tail, position his paws shoulder width apart, and extend his neck as if to say, "Me. Don't forget a biscuit for me."

He pulled up a chair, sat beside Gabriel, and waved his hand in front of the boy's eyes. Not a blink of recognition. Ian grimaced, but dismissed it with a shrug; this was nothing compared to living in his wife's shadow, nothing compared to tailing her during one of her receptions, watching her admirers fawn over her, and look past him. The boy smiled; he seemed mysteriously engaged by another dimension.

Ian pierced the one remaining mango slice with a fork, and lifted it from Gabriel's plate. The boy screamed, banshee-like. Ariana rushed into the dining room. "What are you doing?"

Gabriel's eyelids were clamped shut and his mouth, filled with partially chewed mango, gaped to half the size of his face. "Nooo," he hollered, holding the "o" just as Ariana had done during her voice lessons. He hurled his fork at the glass protecting the family tree, shattering the bottom where his grandmother had embroidered her final entry: Gabriel Ian Ferguson.

"Daddy, give that back to him. You're supposed to help, not make things worse." Ariana scolded as though *he* was the one with the problem.

Ian plopped the stolen fruit in front of Gabriel, landing it with a sloppy smack. The bellowing stopped.

"Everything's okay, Gabriel didn't have to yell," Ariana said, heaping more mango on his plate.

"Don't you see what happened?" Ian asked.

"Yes, and it was cruel."

"No, it was deliberate. I was trying to prove that he's got you trained, and now, he's training me. Just because he doesn't say a lot doesn't mean Gabriel's stupid." Ian paused; Leonora had used similar words after having an argument with their daughter: "Just because your father refuses to play in public doesn't mean he's stopped being a brilliant pianist."

Ariana clamped her hands into fists. "You're right, he's not stupid." She slipped her hand under Gabriel's armpit, and coaxed him from the table. "Time to show Granddaddy what you can do," she said. Hands glistening with juice, he shuffled into the living room, pulled the bench from under the piano, and sat down.

Ian glared at Gabriel's fingerprints on the piano's hand-rubbed, beeswax finish.

"Stand up, Gabriel is too far from the keys," Ariana said, and gave him a nudge. He slid onto his bare feet, his arms rag-doll limp.

"This is ridiculous, his feet don't even touch the pedals. And don't tell me he can read music," Ian said, pointing to his *Etudes* on the music stand.

Ariana slapped the book shut, and handed it to Ian. "Gabriel won't need this."

Clutching his music to his chest, Ian sat on a dining room chair, and scratched his trim beard.

Ariana finished positioning Gabriel. "Go ahead, Gabriel is ready," she said, sliding her hand along the curve of the piano's belly. A wistful expression came over her face. Did she ever think about how different her life would have been had she continued to study with me, Ian wondered? She might have been the one at the piano, rehearsing for her next concert. Ian glanced at his grandson, then at her, and sighed.

Clouds shadowed the room while goldfinches and chickadees sparred for position on the patio feeder. The bell buoy wind chimes sounded. Ian closed his eyes, waited for *Twinkle, Twinkle* or *Mary had a Little Lamb.*

When nothing happened, Ian stood, replaced his *Etudes,* and whisked Gabriel from his bench, suspending him in mid-air. An emptiness he hadn't known since his wife's death seized him and, with it, a new hurt. "We've had our differences, Ariana, and taste in music is one of them, but don't use the boy to mock me. That's cruel," he said. He set Gabriel down, far from his piano.

Gabriel ran back to the dining room, and slithered mango from his plate with an annoying slurp.

"You don't understand, I..." Ariana said, but Ian was already outside, yanking at his tangled garden hose.

That afternoon, Ian opened the package Ariana had left on the dining table. "I'm surprised you were able to get this so soon," he said. "Tripp's usually takes a couple of days to fill custom orders."

"Mr. Tripp stocks that size picture glass, says it's fairly common." Ariana slipped a red rhinestone belt through the loops of her white leather skirt, buckled it, then bent to put on her snakeskin boots. As she tugged, the fringe on her blouse shimmied over her breasts.

Ian grimaced, didn't care for her choice of words. He'd never associated the word "common" with anything this close to the Ferguson name. "That's what you're wearing to an audition?"

"Louie wants someone with a whiny, packed-my-bags-and-left-my-man kind of sound, like mine. This is the look that goes with it."

"Louie?"

"The owner of Texas Louie's, in the Old Port. I met him back home in Kerville. He's the one who convinced me to come east."

"Was that before or after you left Charlie?"

"He's not the reason I left Charlie." She glanced at Gabriel, sitting cross-legged on the living room floor, wiggling his fingers in front of his eyes. "He is. Louie knows a teacher who can help him."

Ian scowled. "I still don't understand who Louie is."

"He's a night-club owner. He's looking for a female singer to make a CD with him."

"Does that mean you wouldn't have to work nights in a smoky bar?"

"It'd be the break I'm looking for." She glanced at her watch. "I'm going to be late. I left Gabriel's tape and the recorder on his cot. He likes to play with his blocks while he listens. I should be back soon." Ariana clicked across the foyer floor. "Wish me luck."

"You don't need luck, you've got your mother's talent."

Ariana turned toward Ian, her amber eyes wide, her pretty lips parted. "That's the nicest thing you've ever said to me."

"I meant to say more, but..." He motioned toward the boxes in the guestroom, then to his feet where Gabriel's blanket lay in a heap. "...I got distracted." His words were supposed to sound upbeat, *vivace,* like they had when he was booking press interviews for Leonora, taking her calls, scheduling her receptions, and trying to convince himself she was the reason he could no longer rehearse for concerts. Without his wife, there was nothing to shield him from—he glanced at Gabriel—mediocrity. His own. He raised his hand and waved.

"Don't forget Gabriel's tape," Ariana said, and slammed the screen door.

The tape recorder lay on the cot between Gabriel's mango-stained pajamas, and an adult-sized T-shirt with "Catch Me If You Can" printed on the front. One ripple of the sheets and Ian found the headset but no tape. He looked under the cot where he found a rabbit with cotton candy-like stuffing bulging from a tear in its neck—a quick repair was all it needed. "I've never been good with a needle and thread," Ian whispered, and peeked in the living room at Gabriel who'd rolled himself in his blanket.

"Oh, dear," Ian said, recalling Gabriel's agitation yesterday in the car. Ian hurried back to the guestroom, and rummaged through a stack of boxes until he found one marked MUSIC. He tore at the masking tape, ripping through a scabby layer of cardboard. There, sealed within their original cellophane wrappers were the CDs he'd sent Ariana: Bach's *Toccata and Fugue*, Mendelssohn's *Andante* and Verdi's *Trovatore*. Beside them, Big Bird, Ernie, and the grungy waif in the trash bin waved from beneath their scratched plastic casing. Surprised at the relief brought on by this gaudy band, Ian popped the tape into the recorder, and hurried into the living room.

"Time for Sesame Street. Okay?"

"Time for Sesame Street. Okay?" Gabriel echoed his words as Ian adjusted his headphones, and pressed *play*. Tinny, barely audible notes escaped from his little earjacks.

"At least it's not country western," Ian said, and ran his fingers through Gabriel's silky curls, the ones he'd inherited from Leonora. "Anyone can see you're a classical man."

When Gabriel seemed content, Ian returned to the guestroom to repack the box. The words, *In recognition for* caught his eye. Beneath it, Ariana's name had been penned in even round letters. He pushed the CDs aside, ran his finger along the glossy laminated finish, traced the gold beveled edges, school seal, and principal's signature, and imagined how grateful the principal must have been to have a powerhouse like Ariana develop a music program for kids like Gabriel.

"That's my girl," he said, nodding his head. He rummaged deeper to find another award, for *Best Female Singer in the Kerville Country Western Sing-Off*, with five gold stars right where they belonged—beside the Ferguson name.

His mouth twisted. He'd received his first and only award when he retired. When it occurred to the Dean of the College of Music that every gifted piano student at the university had competed for the opportunity to sit with Ian on his bench.

Ian picked up a block and remembered Gabriel in the living room. "Here you go, Gabriel," he said, and spilled a basket of bright wooden cubes and rectangles by his bare feet.

"Ohhh nooo," Gabriel cooed, and fluttered his fingers in front of his eyes.

Ian found himself on his hands and knees beside his grandson, sorting blocks into piles. Long rectangles to his left, and short ones to his right. Cubes in the middle. "You can't build bridges if you don't know what you've got for materials," he told him, and handed Gabriel a large red cube. "That'll get you started," he said, and got up with a groan.

Gabriel sniffed the block.

"Would you like me to play for you? This is the ideal situation for the concert pianist who's afraid of crowds." Ian placed one hand on the piano, bowed, then sat on his bench. While Ian was deciding whether to play Debussy or Mozart, Gabriel slipped his headphones off, and stood with the block between his chin and collarbone. Seconds later, he squeezed in between Ian and his piano. Ian smiled.

"If this were a concert, I'd know exactly which pieces I was going to perform. I'd have rehearsed for days, taped myself, critiqued my work, and practiced until I could play the music the way I thought the composer wanted it played." Ian looked at the boy. "Sorry, I don't usually blather like this."

Gabriel moved closer, nuzzled him on his shoulder. Ian flushed with pleasure. "Come sit with your foolish old granddaddy." Gabriel stared at his reflection in the piano's finish, rested his block on the keyboard, and hit a mangled chord.

"I know what you'd like," Ian said, returning the block. He opened the piano bench. "Let's see if I still have it." He hummed a few measures of the Sesame Street theme song, and recalled Ariana playing it.

It'd been years since he rooted through Ariana's music: musty G-clefs, key signatures, and loving directives such as *allegro mais non molto* hovered over flurries of black-flagged notes. Chopin, Beethoven, Bach, Tchaikovsky, Bartok, and Brahams. Buried beneath them, her dog-eared copy of *One Hundred and One Hits for Kids.*

He pressed gently on the spine. When it refused to stay open, Ian weighted it with his *Etudes,* and played. His elegant fingers pranced on the keys while his Hushpuppied feet depressed the damper pedals to prolong the happy sounds.

Nearby, Gabriel twiddled his fingers, and hummed along. Ian's heart swelled. "One more time, my boy?" he asked, and launched a second rendition, this time louder and faster. "*Con gusto*," Ian sang.

"Ohhh nooo." Gabriel leaned backward, lifted both arms above his head and flung his block.

Ian watched it coming toward his piano. His thoughts blurred along with the twisting red projectile and its pointed corners. Ian snatched at the air, but...*twack !* He pushed his bench aside, whipped Gabriel to the other side of the room, hurried back to the piano, and plunged his finger into the gouge, applying pressure as if to his own erupted artery. "Gabriel Ian Ferguson, look what you've done... "

The boy scooped an armful of blocks, flung them into the air, and twirled around and around, waving his skinny arms while chunks of wood rained on his head, and bounced from his shoulders.

Ian clutched his cardigan across his chest and ran into the kitchen. His voice quavered as he spoke into the phone, "Portland. Texas Louie's." He paced. "Yes, it's a business listing."

Before the operator could locate the number, the banshee hooting had stopped. Ian peeked in the living room. Gabriel had seated himself on the piano bench, and was staring, ear pressed to his shoulder, at the damage.

Not wanting to startle him, Ian walked softly through the dining ell, and spoke in a soft shaky tone. "I thought you'd enjoy the fast music. I didn't mean to scare you. Your mother used to laugh when I played like that." He stood where Gabriel could see him and waited. "You're too far away. Let me help you." With one arm cupped around the boy's back, Ian dragged the bench closer to the keyboard.

Gabriel sniffed the keys, and tapped them lightly with his nails.

Ian shuffled through the blocks, sat on a dining room chair, and planted his elbows on his knees. No birds twittered, no squirrels chattered. The bell buoy hung silently. Ian imagined Ariana sitting in place of Gabriel at his piano. Her posture would have been stately, yet at ease, that of a princess on her throne. She'd have exuded poise during the most challenging of pieces. She would never falter, never stop playing, never get up as he once had, and abandon the stage, fingers cramped, notes forgotten, bowels churning with fright. And she would never have to listen to the bewildered hush of the crowd, the haunting silence that hovered in the auditorium until an infuriated patron shattered it with his booing.

But that was years ago, and this was different; it was Gabriel, not Ariana, who'd chosen to sit on his bench, to imitate him. The thought thrilled Ian in a quiet, grandfatherly way and, at the same time, disturbed him, made him feel guilty for clinging to the hope that Ariana would do the same. Leonora's demanding career had been his excuse for not overcoming his fears, for not pursuing his own concert path, but his daughter was different; she had what he lacked—

control and steadiness and the courage to perform. If he told Ariana he felt this way, she'd accuse him of trying to "run her life," just as she'd done before she ran off with Charlie. But it wasn't so; he was just an old man who'd messed up, and didn't want his daughter to do the same. Ian stood. Time to take Gabriel down from his musical crucifix.

As if he'd read Ian's mind, Gabriel positioned his hands on the keyboard, began depressing, lifting, holding, releasing the keys, rhythmically and with spirit. *Con brio.* With an enormous, forgiving spirit. Each simple note hammered at Ian's heart.

He listened for a minute, then had to know. Ian tiptoed into the guestroom, found the box with GABRIEL written on its side, and hurried back to a silent piano. "Was I hallucinating?" he whispered. Gabriel twiddled the keyboard as if nothing had happened.

"That was real, I know it was," Ian shouted, opening the box, and digging through wads of purple tissue paper. At the bottom, a small golden piano gleamed. He lifted his glasses, and inspected the engraving across its top: *Given with special thanks, to Gabriel Ian Ferguson, in appreciation of his extraordinary musical talent. The Kerville Symphony Orchestra.*

Ian lowered himself to the living room floor, guessed that Ariana hadn't told him about her son who, by the age of four, had been recognized as a talent because she wanted to spare him the humiliation. To Ian's surprise, there was none.

An aria-like melody in C sharp minor filled the room. *"Adagio sostenuto,"* Ian whispered. He'd played Beethoven's *Moonlight Sonata* many nights when he and Ariana were alone, and she couldn't sleep. Decades later, this befuddling archangel performed the same dotted rhythms, repeated triplets, and blackened supertonic. His rag-doll muscle tone lessened, and Gabriel seemed to become one with the deaf composer who, during this six minute interval, gave him a way to connect.

Ian closed his blurry eyes and allowed the timelessness of each cadenced measure to collide with his fantasies. Gabriel floated effortlessly beyond his understanding.

The front door slammed. "I thought you were playing," Ariana whispered.

"Is this what you wanted Gabriel to do this morning?" Ian asked, glancing up at her. She nodded, and took Gabriel's award from his hand.

"You wouldn't believe what I had to go through to get the judges to accept a videotape of Gabriel playing. I had to have the psychologist sign a statement saying Gabriel had never played for anyone but me. He wouldn't even play for his father." She lowered herself to the floor, and rested her hand on Ian's knee.

Ian shook his head in disbelief. "How'd he learn to play like this?"

"I taught him every piece you taught me. All I had to do was sit at the piano, play it once, and boom, he locked it in, never forgot it."

Ian listened, relieved that the strain of these past twenty-four hours was being carried away. He thought of earlier years, of the cacophony they'd produced, and how it had been dispelled in this most unexpected of concerti: one that amazed and confounded him with its brilliant patterns and baffling progressions. He thought too, of the countless errors he'd made during those years: as a musician, a husband, and a father. He thought of his grandson, the artistic-autistic, of the debilitating self-consciousness he'd passed on to the boy, and of the genius that offset it. And of Ariana's dedication to Gabriel, and how it reminded him of what he'd felt for her mother, especially during her torturous illness. And how, at the time he'd been convinced his dreams were just that, dreams. Yet, within the safety of this very private concert hall, they were unfolding.

If only Leonora were here, she'd have delighted in this, the most thrilling musical creation of his career: whisper notes. The ones that came in with the evening breezes, scattered remnants of the years, and made room for tomorrow.

UNTIL YOU GET THERE

Overrun with winter-weary North Americans intent on bargain shopping, tanning, and downing rum punch, St. Thomas wasn't Marisa's kind of vacation spot; this excursion had been her husband's idea. For the first couple days, she'd rested by the hotel pool, dog-earring recipe pages in the organic farming magazines that were still addressed to David Nagrom at Windy Way Farm, RR 1, New Jersey. She wrote postcards that sounded as if she'd been airdropped into Sing-Sing, and ripped them in two. She went for short walks. Finally, resigning herself to the real purpose of her trip, she signed up for this tour. Now, she regretted it. David's having manipulated her into coming here was one thing; being intimidated by a feisty tour guide was another.

Marisa disliked the way he called out options for lunch, pursing his lips as if the words fouled his tongue. "Hamburger. Cheeseburger. Mahi-mahi sandwich. Caesar's salad. And this is important—you must specify whether you want pasta salad or fries." The tour guide rested his clipboard on his belt buckle, a green and yellow parrot's head, fixed the point of his pen on the menu, and waited. Carefree vacation chatter fell silent as warblers shot from the morning sky. Huddled around the blue and white *Tour Beautiful St. Thomas* sign, tourists fidgeted with their tickets while Marisa studied the man's amber eyes, self-righteous, ready to mock.

The tour-guide scanned the group. Seconds passed. A round middle-aged woman wearing a T-shirt with "I'm a Survivor of the flood of '95" scrawled across her back stepped forward and cleared her throat. "Two cheeseburgers and one salad," she said.

He glared at her.

Marisa nudged the woman and whispered, "Pasta or fries?"

"Oh yes, two fries, one pasta," the woman said, mouthed "thanks" to Marisa, and scuttled back into the crowd.

The muscles in Marisa's neck tightened. "I'll have a mahi-mahi sandwich – with pasta salad," she said in a quiet voice.

The tour-guide looked up at Marisa. "Thank you for that," he said, pronouncing the nasally *a* sound she was accustomed to hearing as an erudite *ah*. He seemed relieved to have someone who understood his directions. Others inched forward, gave their orders, and stepped aside.

His tally completed, the guide positioned himself between a young black couple and a group of ponytailed teenagers, raised his arm, and dropped it with a slicing motion. He pointed to his right. "This half will ride on the green taxi over there," he said, his square, gold-edged teeth sparkling in the Caribbean sun. Without a moment's hesitation, the designated group gathered their suntan lotions, towels, snorkels, and cameras, and shuffled to the other side of the road.

He pointed to a white Ford with open sides and rows of benches built into its truck bed. "The rest of you go there, make yourselves comfortable. I will see if the owner of this taxi will agree to work for you today." They moved efficiently, hoisting themselves one by one onto the red-striped upholstery.

Seated in the back row on the outside, Marisa lowered her backpack between her knees, and pressed her calves against its rough fabric. The outline of the cardboard box the crematory had shipped a year ago pressed back. Within it, all she had left of David, except his demand, posed as a final request, that she scatter his ashes on St. Thomas. How had David put it? "Upwind of my father's property line." A cluster of palm trees stirred, and a passing breeze cooled the creeping tropical heat. She checked the view to her left and right, then nodded. She'd chosen well; from here she'd be able to see where she was headed, and what she was leaving behind.

Once everyone had settled in, the guide rested his hands on the railing along the truck bed, and studied the solemn faces before him. He leaned forward, as if he was about to share a secret. The hard lines around his mouth softened, and his lips parted like velvety theater curtains. "Good Morning. *Now* we are ready to begin the day on our beautiful island—the island of St. Thomas. I am Charlie...I will be your driver... And for the rest of today...you are Charlie's angels."

Marisa caught the shift in Charlie's tone. The hassle of getting meal orders from vacationing diners completed, he seemed upbeat and gracious. As she found herself forgiving his irascibility—the product of his frustration—the knots along her neck loosened their grip.

"Let me make this the most relaxing, most beautiful day of your vacation. This I will do for you...to do any less would not give you the flavor of our peaceful island." Charlie's pauses reminded her of Paul Harvey, the noon radio show she'd listened to while warming broth for David to sip through a flexible red-striped straw. By then, the hepatitis had nearly destroyed his liver.

Charlie opened his arms and made a huge swooping motion as if to embrace the island and present it, dripping with warm salty water, to his angels. He leaned back, closed his eyes and filled his lungs. "Yes, my friends...breathe our island air...let it refresh...and purify you."

Marisa's neck threatened to tighten again—the word "purify" brought her back to a particularly frustrating afternoon with David. "My father's a doctor, he had to suspect I was a carrier, and he never said a word, not one word." She reminded David this was nothing new; he'd been at odds with his father since he was a boy. She confessed that had she been in his father's position, after David had had his accident she, too, would have given him five units of island blood, despite the possibility of its being contaminated. "What did you expect your father to do? He found his eighteen-year old son at the bottom of a ravine. Filtered blood wasn't available. You're blaming him for something that happened twenty-six years ago." Long after David had given up chugging rum, and open-throttling his Harley along St. Thomas' dangerous winding roads.

She took a breath and, expelling it, recalled the many times she'd tried to get her husband to ease up on his father. David had the habit of studying his soil-crusted nails whenever he spoke about the man he'd disappointed: "Not until he respects me for the work *I've* chosen. Marrying you was the only thing he said I did right." Propped in the corner of the sofa, the position Marisa came to associate with his deterioration, David would slip his wire-rims to the tip of his long nose, straighten an imaginary bow tie, and imitate his father's patrician accent. "The brightest scientist—hematologists from Sweden, bio-oncologists from Austria, PhDs from Canada travel to my laboratories, but *my* son is so busy on his farm, he doesn't have time to visit."

Charlie started the truck, and drove past the shops in downtown Charlotte Amalie. The loudspeaker clicked on. "I want you to experience the fragrances surrounding those of us who live on this island. No doubt, you are familiar with the famous designer perfume shops that grace the streets of this, the capital of St. Thomas. These are not the fragrances I will share with you."

From Main Street, Charlie turned onto a narrow ribbon of faded road. "St. Thomas measures fifteen hundred and fifty feet at its highest point. Not that high, you may think, until you realize our island was created by a volcanic eruption that cooled into a steep, narrow mass—thirteen miles long and three miles wide. Then you will understand why my grandfather's family traveled on donkeys along the pathways we now use as roads," Charlie said.

The taxi's movement pressed Marisa against the seat. Perspiration dampened her short hair, collected at the corners of her forehead, rolled down the hollow of her cheeks. She clutched the edge of the cushion. Her neck strained against the force pushing her backward toward the heart-shaped rear window that had framed many honeymooning couples. She hated these twisting, winding heights; they reminded her of David's recklessness, of how it had destroyed his life, and hers.

The taxi followed the spiraling pitch around a corner. Marisa gasped. If she'd been driving, she'd have stopped, left the keys in the ignition, and made her way back to the gentle coast. Charlie pressed upward along the edge of the cliff. She peeked at the taxi's back wheels. They cornered as effortlessly as the wheels David had rigged on his wagon, the one he'd built to fit between his rows of meticulously tended herbs and vegetables. From them, he would select glossy eggplants, and bouquets of basil-laced lettuce for her to prepare at the restaurant she'd named after him: David's Landing.

A driveway dipped deep into a patchy yard where a rooster strutted alongside a low-roofed eatery. Charlie pulled over and stepped out. Tucked far below within a mountainous elbow was a tree-lined harbor where white sailboats skimmed the turquoise water. Cameras clicked and whirred. Frenzy over, the tourists returned to their seats. A bird trilled high and sweet. "May I introduce the official greeter of the Virgin Islands, the bananaquit," Charlie said, as a small, yellow-breasted bird darted among crimson hibiscus flowers. "He's searching for sweet nectar, just as we're looking for sweet smells." Charlie picked a shiny leaf from a lollypop-shaped tree, crushed it, and brought it to his nose. "Ah...this fragrance you will surely recognize as lime." He handed it to a man in a Gold's Gym muscle shirt, waited while he sniffed. "How about this one?" Charlie asked, reaching around the muscle man, handing a chubby redhead a larger, shinier leaf.

Like one of the spoiled rich kids at Camp Minhatulo, the summer science camp where David and Marisa had met, the redhead took the second leaf, rolled her eyes, and passed it to Marisa. Marisa crushed the leaf and breathed its aroma. "Mmm," she murmured, entranced by the cinnamon burst not found in the herbs that grew in New Jersey soil. She sniffed again, and thought of David, tanned and strong, on his knees in the sandy loam, planting herbs he'd raised from seed, herbs she would stir into the eclectic array of entrees David's Landing had become known for. She looked at Charlie and shook her head in amazement. "What is this?"

"That, my dear lady, is bay leaf."

She had the sensation of stepping over a familiar threshold, but seeing the room for the first time. "Bay? The bay leaf I buy doesn't have a smell. Come to think of it, it doesn't taste like much either. I use it because the recipe calls for it. Quite frankly, Charlie, I've been tempted not to use it at all."

Marisa was standing now, clutching the bay leaf in her fist, speaking in tones that were loud, and clear, and indignant. And didn't she have a right? To think she'd been buying dried bay leaves ever since she made her first roux twenty-five years ago. She stopped; the others were listening, admiring the confidence David had almost robbed her of. She held the bay leaf to her nose. Sniffing the aroma of the herb she'd thought of as dead rather than dried, excited her and filled her with hope—something that had died along with David. She continued speaking to the group even though, had anyone asked, she would have confessed it was Charlie in whom she was confiding. "After this, I'm going to look for fresh bay leaf—I'll never use dried again." Charlie beamed, seemed to understand this was no casual vow.

At that moment, a flock of parrots flew by. "Look," someone shouted as a blur of royal blues, lime greens, deep yellows, and reds whirred alongside the taxi. "Did you see that?" the man in the Gold's Gym muscle shirt cried out.

"I never seen a parrot outside a pet store or a zoo. Praise be, they are truly a gift from the Lord," said an obese woman with exotic plaits and gold sphinx earrings. She grabbed hold of the back of her seat and twisted toward Marisa. "You so right about them lousy dried spices they pawn off on us back in the states. I kill myse'f trying to make good tastin' dishes for him..." —she pointed to the thin mustached man beside her—"...and they still don't taste no good. Now I know why."

Charlie started the taxi and pulled out onto the vertical roadway. The woman lurched sideways, almost crushing her companion. Marisa popped a mint in her mouth, hoping to ease her queasiness. Charlie's voice came over the loudspeaker. "Now I will take you to the most scenic view on St. Thomas. From here you will be able to take photos of our beautiful Virgin Islands."

Marisa lingered as the others edged their way through the parking lot toward the observation deck. David and his family had flown here to their mountain farmhouse every year during school vacations. An island couple, Martin and Yolanda, whom David nicknamed MY, cared for the farm and him, too. Years later, when Dr. Nagrom retired, he moved to his farmhouse, fired MY, and replaced them with his housekeepers from Annapolis.

Marisa stood on the seat to get a better view. So this was where David wanted his ashes scattered, the place he'd written about in his diary where *Islands jut like stems/Beneath goblets of cloud-mist/emptiness contained.*

Haiku had given David solace while Marisa badgered him about undergoing a liver transplant. "If Mickey Mantle used his connections to get a transplant, why shouldn't you?" she'd argued. But he refused to ask for his father's help, didn't seem to understand that if he died, part of her would too.

Early in their marriage, when they'd placed a bid on Windy Way Farm, she realized how tied to David she'd become. He'd been so excited, he couldn't stop talking about the sellers, an elderly couple, who said David and Marisa were "impressive." That their desire to be self-sufficient was key to running a farm. If only they knew Marisa's enthusiasm wasn't a reflection of independence; it mirrored the opposite. She'd read it took eight years to recover from the death of a spouse. Would eight years be enough, she wondered? She traced the fine lines and dings on the heart-shaped window at the back of Charlie's truck, and sighed.

Charlie came toward her. "Are you worried about leaving your things?" he asked. She nodded. "Many travelers are unsure of what to do with their valuables," he said.

"I've been struggling with that quite some time."

"Come, I will watch your backpack. Nothing will happen to it, I promise." He offered her his hand. She balanced herself against the warmth and sturdiness of his thick palm, stepped from the running board to the ground, and murmured her thanks for helping her. Again.

Within minutes, she was shouldering her way among clicking cameras, through throngs of dazed tourists, toward the far end of the observation deck. "So many people," Marisa said to the woman in the survivor T-shirt.

"Mind taking our picture?" the woman asked, handing Marisa her camera. "By the way, I'm Shelly, this is my husband, James, and our son, Timmy."

Marisa introduced herself, took the camera, and centered the family in the viewfinder. They seemed so small against the endless blue sky and lush green islands that Marisa moved closer, and focused on Shelly's husband with his blanched hair and vacant blue eyes. Their teenaged son folded his arms across his chest and turned away. "Everyone ready?" Marisa called out.

"Timmy?" Shelly asked, motioning for him to stand in front of his father's limp left arm. The flash of impatience in her eyes said he knew darn well what she expected him to do.

Timmy's oversized shorts rested low on his lanky trunk, revealing skull and crossbones boxers clinging to his hips. "I don't want to pose for a stupid picture. And I don't like standing here," he said, nodding his shaved head toward his father.

"Swap places with me," Shelly said. "And hurry, Marisa's waiting." She turned to her husband. "James, smile so we can show everyone back home what a happy time we're having." With that, she pushed her sunglasses on top of her frizzy gray hair. "No one thought I'd corral these two long enough to pull this one off," she said to Marisa, curling one hand around her husband's left arm, and smiling as if her life was one never-ending holiday.

Marisa zoomed in on this woman, so much like herself, the perpetuator of the happiness-despite-reality myth that had buoyed her during David's years as president of the Northeast Organic Farmers' Association, presenter at their annual conference, columnist for *The Organic Newsletter,* and collaborator with the Department of Agriculture. Marisa dismissed his constant activity as though it were a pesky gnat. She kissed David goodbye before he left for his association meeting, the night the Chamber of Commerce was to honor her with its Distinguished Entrepreneur Award. She wished she'd paid more attention to the stress the photographer had captured in her smile. Marisa's hand was trembling. She steadied the viewfinder against her cheek and snapped the picture.

"How about you, honey? Can I take a picture for you?" Shelly asked.

Marisa handed her the plastic camera she'd bought in the hotel convenience store, and exchanged places with the family. Shelly looked around. "By yourself?" she asked.

Marisa nodded, forced a smile. "My father-in-law lives on the island."

"I meant, is your hubby with you?"

"You could say that."

Shelly looked around as if she expected David to join them. When he didn't, she shrugged, and took Marisa's picture. "We're going home tomorrow. How about you?" she asked, returning the camera. Marisa nodded. "After I almost messed up the lunch count, Timmy said it was just our luck to spend on our last day with a Nazi like Charlie."

"Charlie was a bit edgy. I used to get like that after staying up all night with my sick husband," Marisa said.

"You too, huh? Listen hon, I know exactly what you're going through," Shelly leaned toward Marisa, her stale cigarette breath filling the space between them. "After Timmy, I never thought I'd have to change diapers or bathe anyone else—until James' stroke." She cracked a small ironic smile, and walked toward her husband, then turned around. "Don't forget, it could be worse. How worse, you'll never know, until you get there."

Marisa agreed. She'd divided the last twenty-seven years into three parts: the first, where glossy black and white prints of her holding her award, hung in the den beside David's citations for his "Tireless contributions to the Future Organic Farmers Club of America;" the second, the undocumented world of David's illness. Alone in the third, she often returned to the den for assurance that life hadn't always seemed this surreal. Losing David was one thing; learning she'd contracted his disease was another.

Marisa followed Shelly and her husband back to the taxi. True to his word, Charlie stood guard, his taupe and black print shirt luffing softy around his firm middle, his collar open to tiny gray hairs huddled like sheep against his chest. When the group had reassembled, Charlie propped his foot on the running board, and waited until they fixed their collective eye on him. In his soft bass voice, he told the story of the sugar cane plantations, and slavery before the emancipation, and of the rebellion that followed. His words glistened like the islands of perspiration forming along his temples. Marisa leaned toward him, straining to understand. "But that was back in 1733," he said. His wistful smile implied disappointment at not having been there to fight for the freedom he now enjoyed.

Charlie went on to explain that the United States had bought St. Thomas, St. Croix, and St. John's from Denmark for the grand price of three hundred dollars an acre, and that he and his fellow islanders were flourishing in their status as a U.S. territory. Marisa scowled. Territory—as in under the influence of a higher authority? That's how she felt when David had extracted his awful promise from her. That's how she continued to feel. Not that she objected to his wish to be cremated, although the thought of fire consuming his flesh still made her shudder. And she didn't mind scattering his ashes on the island where he'd spent his boyhood vacations. But to ask her to do so upwind of his father's property, where his ashes would make landfall on his father's patio, gardens, his afternoon cocktail...

She wondered if she could pick a few sprigs of the aromatic bay leaf, bring them home and grind them into a potion that would neutralize the odor of a dead man's bitterness. Even if she managed to get the organic matter past the sniffing beagles of US Customs, what difference would it make? She took a deep breath. Her nostrils twitched with the memory of David's sour smell as she watched over him from the worn chintz chair by his side of their bed. His face contorted and relaxed with the pain's press and release. She told herself when David passed, so too would his bitterness. How could she have been so wrong?

Marisa studied Charlie's smile, and wondered if living in a territorial paradise satisfied him. What had his journey been like before he'd achieved the status of spokesman for the status quo? Had he been one of the laborers in David's photographs? One who rose before dawn to build rich men's homes and, at week's end, bet his paycheck on games of dominoes played under the ragged shade of a tamarind tree?

Such were the photos David had taken years ago of men and women huddled outside shanty bars, broken chairs scattered beneath strings of gloomy lights hanging along dusty driveways. "These were my father's builders, gardeners, housekeepers, and cooks. I swam and fished with their sons, listened to their wives tell stories, while my father entertained his precious colleagues. These are the sights the guides won't show the ordinary tourist," he'd told her. Marisa rested her hand on her backpack; she didn't consider herself an ordinary tourist.

Charlie drove the taxi downhill while describing their destination—a sheltered cove on the north side of the island. "We will have our lunch on a quiet beach, in no ordinary restaurant," he said over the loudspeaker. "The Parrot Fish Grill belongs to my daughter, who has an apron waiting for me in the kitchen." The group laughed. "I am happy to take my place at the grill, so you will enjoy a delicious hot meal." Charlie turned left at an intersection, one so tight he had to back up before he could get enough clearance to make the hairpin turn. Other drivers watched, and when he drove off, waved and tooted their horns.

Such was the support Marisa had known while running her restaurant. When word got out she planned to close David's Landing, her friends and neighbors offered to run it until David got better. Only a few knew his condition was irreversible, fewer knew she had contracted his disease, a mild form in its early stages and oh, so much more treatable. She would live, her doctors said, but the Department of Health and Sanitation would never renew her license. Would never allow her to prepare meals for her patrons, the townspeople who returned week after week, who recommended her to friends willing to wait in line to get in.

A dense mass of competing branches, brambles, and broken trunks protruding from the mossy forest floor enclosed the narrow road. A canopy of unruly trees reached beyond the forest's chaos, blotted the sky, and camouflaged the ocean. Theirs was the only taxi traveling down the bumpy, unpaved road. Marisa clamped her calves around her backpack to keep it from jiggling. Charlie stopped, and pointed out a huge brown goiter surrounding the mid-section of a tree. "That, my friends, is a termite's nest," he said. The group gasped. "Now you understand why we build our homes with stucco rather than wood." He laughed, and drove off, seeming more light-hearted than before. "I am concentrating so much on what I must do at the grill, that I almost forgot to tell you...I have phoned and asked my daughter to prepare a complimentary rum punch for you…'Charlie's angels are thirsty,' I told her."

As the road opened onto a sandy apron by the bay, a bouncy reggae tune came over the loudspeaker. Shelly swayed with the gentle beat, bumping her husband to one side, and her son on the other. The muscle T-shirt stood, clapping his hands overhead. His red-haired girlfriend wiggled beside him. The woman with the plaits put her jiggling arm around her husband, and stroked his neck. Marisa tapped her foot, recalled the last barn dance she and David had attended. He wanted to do the two-step, and Marisa wanted to lead. "This is dancing—the man has to lead," he told her. "Sexist notion," she replied with a laugh, unaware that within months a silent bandit would steal his lead, and deliver it, tattered, to her.

Charlie parked the taxi in the parking lot's last available space, and announced that after lunch they would be free to enjoy the secluded beach—swim, sunbathe, snorkel, or walk the shoreline. "Because the Parrot Grill is a small establishment, you must leave your belongings in the taxi. And please, don't worry, this is a safe place, no harm will come to your things." The speaker clicked off, and Charlie rushed into the grill.

Marisa found herself wishing she'd taken the half-day tour; traveling alone was tiring, and difficult, and the day had started to drag. But the half-day tour didn't go to the highest scenic ledge on St. Thomas, and that was what she'd wanted to see. At sunset, she planned to hire a real taxi to take her there. She patted the fifty-dollar bill she'd tucked in her pocket to cover the fare.

Last to step beneath the grill's thatched roof, Marisa searched for a seat. Arranged around a U-shaped bar were clusters of round tables occupied by tourists, many she'd never seen before. Even the barstools were taken. Marisa felt out of place with these strangers, these couples, this vacationing. Charlie's reggae music was playing, but Charlie was nowhere to be seen. She needed a few moments to collect herself. No one would notice if she returned to the taxi.

She was about to leave when someone tapped her shoulder. She turned around. "We saved you a seat," Timmy said. With his sullen expression and odd clothing, he could have passed for David, thirty-five years ago. The boy pointed to a small table by the kitchen door.

Shelly leaned—half-sitting, half-standing—against the wall, and waved. Marisa raised her hand. By the time she and Timmy edged their way across the room, Shelly had just finished slicing her husband's cheeseburger in half and was setting his plate in front of him. She popped a few fries in her mouth. "I thought I was going to have to eat alone," Marisa said. Shelly swallowed. "Not while we're here," she said, piling lettuce and tomato on her cheeseburger.

Timmy plopped on the stool beside his mother. He speared the lettuce on his plate with his fork, and flicked off crumbles of cheese with his stubby, chewed nails.

"What's the matter, hon?" Shelly asked.

Timmy scowled. "Salad's loaded with this stuff." He lifted a chunk of white cheese and dropped it.

"Here, take some of my fries." His mother pointed to her half-eaten pile.

"You're kiddin'—a place like this has gotta use animal fat."

Marisa looked at Shelly. "Vegan?" she asked, lifting a forkful of pasta salad.

Shelly nodded. Her husband chewed on his cheeseburger, his eyes reflecting none of his son's distress. Timmy continued picking out the cheese, setting it aside. He scrubbed his hands on his napkin. "There's no way I can eat this," he said, crumbling the napkin and tossing it on the table. Marisa glanced at the porthole in the kitchen door, at Charlie's glare.

The door swung open. Charlie tossed his grease-stained apron into the kitchen, and stepped out into the noisy room. The door pivoted until a woman's small face appeared on the other side of the porthole. Her round, anxious eyes followed Charlie as he approached Timmy. "Is something wrong with your salad, my man?" he asked. Marisa and Shelly exchanged glances.

Timmy pushed his plate towards Charlie. "This has cheese, and I don't eat cheese."

"It's feta," Charlie said, with a shrug. "It's good for you."

"Take it away."

Charlie's mouth twisted into a scornful smile. "No need to be so upset, my friend. You've picked most of it off." Timmy stared past his mother, and balled his hands into fists. "Now,

now, none of that," Charlie said, clicking his tongue. "I will bring your salad into the kitchen, and rinse it off for you." He tilted his head, looked down at the boy who stared at the table, then whisked the plate away.

Shelly turned to Marisa. "What did I tell you? The guy's a Nazi."

Shelly's words hurt, as if they'd been directed at her. For some inexplicable reason, Charlie had become important to Marisa. Not in any future-oriented romantic way; he was the kind of stranger who appears after your car breaks down on a deserted back road, and you're about to panic. You're wary at first, until you realize he means you no harm, and he understands cars.

Marisa lifted the top of her roll. The mahi-mahi was lightly breaded, golden brown, with the thinnest slice of grilled lemon, and wilted thyme. This was Charlie's work, created within his daughter's kitchen. Could anyone with this sense of delicacy be as horrible as Shelly maintained?

James was getting up from the table. Shelly fingered a cigarette and her lighter, and followed him. "Dad and I are going to the beach. We'll be right back, okay, sweetie?"

Timmy grimaced, nodded, and watched his parents make their way across the room. A large noisy group had gathered around the bar and was ordering another round of drinks. The Gold's Gym muscle-shirt was gulping beer, and taking bets on how long it would take the bananaquit that had just landed to peck a hole in a small package of sugar. The wait staff filtered through the grill, clearing paper plates, washing tabletops, unscrewing the heads from the parrot salt and pepper shakers, and refilling them.

Marisa thought about Shelly's comment. It wasn't that Marisa excused Charlie's behavior; she didn't. And Timmy's rudeness didn't help. Yet, if this had been her grill, she would have avoided the unpleasantness by going into the kitchen, and combining an assortment of garden fresh veggies into an elaborate vegan platter, sending it out to the boy, free of charge. That was her problem, David used to say—she went out of her way to make others feel good, even when they were the ones in the wrong.

Within minutes, the kitchen door inched open, and Charlie returned with a fresh, cheese-free salad, a basket of warm rolls, and a meek expression. "Here you are, my man. Enjoy," he said, glancing back at his daughter, who leaned against the kitchen door with her arms folded across her chest. Piled high on her head, and secured within an orange and blue bandana, her dreadlocks bobbed as she nodded at him.

Charlie cocked his head and watched the boy fill his mouth and chew, as if no one was standing beside him. Charlie waited, and when the boy continued to eat without saying a word, headed for one of the clean tables, and sat down. Moments later, his daughter appeared with a huge platter, and placed it before her father. She took a pitcher of water from the bar, and poured him a glass. With one hand on the table, and the other on his shoulder, she smiled a soft smile, whispered a few words in his ear then disappeared into the kitchen.

"How's your salad?" Marisa asked Timmy.

"Okay."

"Is it better?"

"Yeah, much better."

"I think Charlie got in trouble for not helping you sooner."

"He deserved it." Timmy said, spearing a tomato. "They should have laws against letting geeks like him out in public. I can't wait to go home and be with normal people."

Marisa didn't want to listen to any more. She excused herself, and headed across the room toward Charlie. Hunched over his platter, his forearms resting on the edge of the table, he ripped a crust of bread, soaked it in salad dressing, placed it in his mouth and, as he chewed, starting ripping another chunk of bread.

Charlie looked up at her and swallowed. "How was your meal?"

"I saw what happened. You did a good thing. The boy's pretty angry about his Dad."

A puzzled expression came over Charlie's sad face. He set the chunk of bread on the edge of his plate. "How? How do you know?"

Marisa focused for a moment on the black-and-white striped head of the bananaquit, flitting from table to table. "He reminds me of my husband—angry about something his father couldn't control."

Charlie sighed. "I shouldn't lose my temper over a spoiled kid wasting food, but I remember our relatives gathering right there, outside the shack we grew up in..." He pointed to the parking lot. "When my father could afford to, he slaughtered a chicken, and we celebrated. My mother chopped enough vegetables and potatoes to make a pot of stew that would feed all of us." He turned his head toward the parking lot and blinked. "My wife died two years ago. She gave me the gift of a daughter to keep me civil. Without her, where would I be?"

Marisa searched his face for the angry winches that had twisted his mouth into a sneer, and found the relief of a man gently contained. Marisa imagined her father-in-law's long, tight face and intense eyes softened by a dose of Charlie's brand of relief. She imagined herself going to the home he'd built on the north side of the island, not far from where David wanted his ashes scattered, and inviting him to join her in fulfilling his son's final request. She fingered the fifty-dollar bill in her pocket.

"Charlie? Do me a favor?"

He rubbed his face and leaned toward her.

"Drive me to the top of the island at sunset today? There's something I want to do." She withdrew her hand from her pocket and, with it, a crushed leaf.

"I see you still have my bay leaf," Charlie said.

Marisa thought of Charlie's confidence as he pressed upward on the spiraling island roads. How he, like the lone bananaquit, believed this craggy volcanic remnant of an island would nourish him with its sweet nectar, purify him with its air. She sniffed the bay leaf, inhaling the scent that had neutralized the odor of David's bitterness. "It hasn't lost its fragrance. It never will."

ACKNOWLEDGMENTS

In writing *Small Lies,* I aimed to create a journal using the short-story form. The ideas for the stories in this collection came from personal, local, and international events that whirled around me during the later part of the twentieth century and early years of the twenty-first. Some stories found inspiration in newspaper articles, a few germinated within miles of my home, and others originated in observations that struck me while traveling. When the universality of the untruths the characters relied on emerged as the collection's underlying theme, I was intrigued by the ways in which those characters made peace within their lives.

While working on these stories, I was blessed with the support and guidance of fellow writers and teachers at Stonecoast Writers Conference. I send special thanks to Patricia McNair, Jack Driscoll, Debra Sparks, Michael White, and Lee Hope for their insight and encouragement. I cherish the memories of the hours spent with Nancy Barbe, Jean Aberlin, Janet Albright, Harriet Frazier (sadly, deceased), Kathleen Harper, and Jean Sheridan—the writing group born of shared Stonecoast experiences.

Since that time, during these post-Stonecoast decades, I've been fortunate to have Carol Semple and Frazier Meade as writing partners. I treasure the insights, compassion, humor, and friendship our trio has shared these many years.

I am fortunate to have the best of publishing teams: Betty Darby, my copy-editor, nothing misses your fine editorial eye! Angela and Richard Hoy, Ali Hibberts, Brian Whiddon, Todd Engel, and all the talented staff at Booklocker, you have become part of my writing family. Caitlin Hamilton Summie, publicist, thank you for guiding me with your insights as I make my way along this important chapter in my publishing journey.

As always, my love and gratitude to Mike, my husband and supporter, who continues to inspire me in countless ways.

ABOUT THE AUTHOR

Photo by Lesley MacVane

Catherine Gentile's fiction received the Dana Award for Short Fiction, and achieved finalist status in the American Fiction Prize Contest, The Ledge, and the International Reynolds Price Short Fiction Award. Her short fiction was chosen as semifinalist in the Boston Fiction Festival, and the New Millennium Writing Competition. After publishing in *American Fiction*, *The Briar Cliff Review*, *The Chaffin Journal* and others, Catherine ventured into the world of the novel.

Her debut novel, *The Quiet Roar of a Hummingbird*, achieved finalist status in the Eric Hoffer Novel Award for Excellence in Independent Publishing.

Catherine's non-fiction has appeared in *Writers' Market*, *North Dakota Quarterly*, *Down East*, and *Maine Magazine*. She has contributed to numerous online publications including: *Garden Write Now!*, *Ezine.com*, and *Portland Trails Newsletter*, and has published a non-fiction ebook, *The Caregiver's Journey: Tools, Tips, and Provisions.*

Catherine currently edits a monthly newsletter entitled, *Together With Alzheimer's*, which has subscribers throughout the United States.

Her second novel, *Sunday's Orphan,* is scheduled for publication in fall, 2021.

A native of Hartford, Connecticut, Catherine lives with her husband and muse on a small island off the coast of Maine.

Catherine invites you to explore her website: www.catherinegentile.com. She welcomes select invitations for readings and speaking engagements. Contact her via email: catgen207@gmail.com.

CPSIA information can be obtained
at www.ICGtesting.com
Printed in the USA
BVHW030315121120
593151BV00019B/62